# SASKATCHEWAN HOCKEY
The Game of Our Lives

Edited by
Allan Safarik

MacIntyre Purcell Publishing Inc.

Copyright 2018 Allan Safarik

All rights reserved. No part of this book covered by the copyrights hereon may be reproduced or used in any form or by any means – graphic, electronic, or mechanical – without the prior written permission of the publisher. Any request for photocopying, recording, taping, or information storage and retrieval systems of any part of this book shall be directed in writing to the Canadian Reprography Collective, 379 Adelaide Street, West, Suite M1, Toronto, Ontario, M5V 1S5.

MacIntyre Purcell Publishing Inc.
194 Hospital Rd.
Lunenburg, Nova Scotia
B0J 2C0
(902) 640-3350

www.macintyrepurcell.com
info@macintyrepurcell.com

Printed and bound in Canada by Friesens

Design and layout: Alex Hickey
Cover design: Denis Cunningham
Front cover photo: Permission to use the image "Practising For the Game" by Allen Sapp is granted by the Estate of Allen Sapp.

ISBN: 978-1-77276-110-8

Library and Archives Canada Cataloguing in Publication

    Saskatchewan hockey anthology / edited by Allan Safarik.

ISBN 978-1-77276-110-8 (softcover)

    1. Hockey stories, Canadian (English)--Saskatchewan.
2. Canadian fiction (English)--21st century. I. Safarik, Allan, 1948-, editor

PS8323.H62S28 2018    C813'.60803579    C2018-904143-9

MacIntyre Purcell Publishing Inc. would like to acknowledge the financial support of the Government of Canada and the Nova Scotia Department of Tourism, Culture and Heritage.

# Mr. Hockey

Photo by Landon Johnson

In 2005, the statue of Gordie Howe by sculptor Michael Martin was moved from the southwest corner of 20th Street and First Avenue in Saskatoon to the main entrance at SaskTel Centre, home of the WHL Saskatoon Blades. In keeping with Howe's last wishes, the ashes of Gordie and his wife Colleen were interred in 2016 in the base of Howe's statue.

In memory of Dolores Reimer

# Table of Contents

Mr. Hockey .................................................. 3

Introduction .................................................. 11

Old Hockey Skates ........................................... 15
  Glen Sorestad

Hockey Night ................................................ 16
  Robert Currie

Hockey Nights in Canada .................................... 17
  Mansel Robinson

Anecdote of the Hockey Game ............................... 20
  Gerald Hill

Breakaway ................................................... 21
  Maureen Ulrich

In Plain Sight ................................................ 23
  William Robertson

My First Hockey Service ..................................... 25
  Mick Burrs

At the Arena ................................................. 27
  Kelley Jo Burke

Autumn 1972 ................................................ 29
  Randy Lundy

Wreck League ............................................... 35
  Stephen Scriver

The Shut Out ................................................ 37
  Dolores Reimer

Once Is Once Too Many .................................46
*Stephen Scriver*

Goalie .................................................49
*Rudy Thauberger*

Going Down............................................54
*Stephen Scriver*

Stanislowski Vs. Grenfell...............................55
*Stephen Scriver*

Indian Head, Saskatchewan............................57
*Bill Boyd*

Hockey Lesson ........................................62
*Robert Currie*

Beneath the Frozen Moon .............................63
*Robert Currie*

The Hockey Game .....................................65
*Wes Fineday*

Northland Pro .........................................71
*Gary Hyland*

The B-P-T .............................................72
*Gary Hyland*

The Reluctant Black Hawk .............................75
*Brenda Zeman*

Old-Timers Hockey ....................................98
*Glen Sorestad*

The Northfield Comets ................................103
*Allan Safarik*

Gordie's Floral Sky ....................................118
*Don Kerr*

Gordie Howe Statue, Saskatoon . . . . . . . . . . . . . . . . . . . . . . . . .120
*Myrna Garanis*

The Woman Behind the Mask . . . . . . . . . . . . . . . . . . . . . . . . . . .121
*Calvin Daniels*

Canadian Angels. . . . . . . . . . . . . . . . . . . . . . . . . . . . . . . . . . . . . . .135
*Lorna Crozier*

Saskatchewan's Own Golden Girls. . . . . . . . . . . . . . . . . . . . . . .137
*Calvin Daniels*

Art Is International and Has No Borders . . . . . . . . . . . . . . . . . 144
*Don Kerr*

Bienfait, Saskatchewan . . . . . . . . . . . . . . . . . . . . . . . . . . . . . . . .147
*Bill Boyd*

Johnny . . . . . . . . . . . . . . . . . . . . . . . . . . . . . . . . . . . . . . . . . . . . . .154
*Stephen Scriver*

Max Bentley and the Hockey Pants . . . . . . . . . . . . . . . . . . . . .157
*Robert Currie*

Farm Team . . . . . . . . . . . . . . . . . . . . . . . . . . . . . . . . . . . . . . . . . .166
*Laurie Muirhead*

Aboriginal Title Comes to a Young Team . . . . . . . . . . . . . . . .167
*Calvin Daniels*

Another Colour Man . . . . . . . . . . . . . . . . . . . . . . . . . . . . . . . . . .172
*William Robertson*

End of the Season. . . . . . . . . . . . . . . . . . . . . . . . . . . . . . . . . . . . .174
*William Robertson*

A Hall of Our Own. . . . . . . . . . . . . . . . . . . . . . . . . . . . . . . . . . . . .175
*Darrell Davis*

Bios. . . . . . . . . . . . . . . . . . . . . . . . . . . . . . . . . . . . . . . . . . . . . . . . . .187

Permissions . . . . . . . . . . . . . . . . . . . . . . . . . . . . . . . . . . . . . . . . . .193

Acknowledgements . . . . . . . . . . . . . . . . . . . . . . . . . . . . . . . . . . .195

# Introduction

Putting together a literary anthology about hockey in Saskatchewan has been an enlightening experience. In gathering the material together, mostly out of print sources discovered in libraries and book dealers' catalogues, it quickly became obvious that a small pool of writers throughout the decades were responsible for producing a rich body of work from the grassroots in a province that has embraced the game in a most unique manner. This anthology is a sampler of the wide range of work they have accomplished with their love for the game that is their passion and the passion of their countrymen. Every writer in this anthology has been profoundly influenced by "the game of our lives," the subtitle a friend recommended to me as an appropriate summing up of this collection, *Saskatchewan Hockey*.

I have heard it said that hockey is a religion in Saskatchewan. I won't go that far. However, I will say that hockey is celebrated in this province in a way that is perhaps unequalled anywhere else. The small population of approximately a million people in a vast agriculture - and natural resources - rich land are a people who have embraced the game as if it were their own pastime that is played informally on roads, in barnyards, schoolyards, basements, on sloughs, potholes, backyard rinks, outdoor rinks and in hallways and lobbies (with mini sticks) in the myriad of towns, villages, hamlets, First Nations communities and farms that cover the province, as well as in the cities.

There is barely a town that does not have a rink, some with ice-making equipment, others relying on natural ice that sets when the lines are put down, the rink is flooded and the doors are left open to allow frigid air to do the job. The rinks that abound in nearly every community in the province are an odd collection of buildings that reflect the eccentricities of the decades.

Some are regulation size, others are short and narrow or have extremely low ceilings. Roof lines are as individual as the collective imagination has allowed. There are often overhangs or poop decks, and lobbies, concessions, dressing rooms and viewing areas follow no conformity. That is not to say that there aren't state-of-the-art rinks all over the province, especially in the larger communities and in the cities. Minor hockey, senior hockey, women's hockey, old-timers hockey and rec hockey abound wherever there are rinks and a variety of skill levels and leagues occur wherever the game is played.

Saskatchewan is a harsh landscape for much of the year. Spring and fall are generally short and are often eventful according to the whims of the weather. Summer is short and sweet on the prairies. The corn in the garden seems to tremble and grow before the eyes as the sun lures the stalks into the sky. The winter, which often takes up the better part of seven months, is an austere time when the mercury can drop lower than 40 below zero and stay there for weeks. The common fact in Saskatchewan is that rinks are social places where families gather and come and go according to practice or game schedules. Often the busiest place in town is the rink, which is easily found because in winter it is generally surrounded by parked and idling vehicles.

People in Saskatchewan are robust and energetic. They get out and go to work and get their chores and obligations done no matter what the weather brings. In the winter, the rink is full of rink rats who go there for exercise, sport, companionship and entertainment. Rural children in Saskatchewan often ride buses back and forth to school. Sometimes they travel long distances to school during the week and take long rides by vehicle or bus to play hockey in faraway towns in the evening or on weekends, often on bad roads in appalling weather conditions.

Everywhere seems far away in Saskatchewan. People are used to taking the long drive to get the mail or pick up groceries in a larger centre, or travel for a hundred kilometres or more for a minor hockey league game or to follow the local senior team when it is on the road. These distances grow longer when the provincial playoffs begin or when teams travel for tournaments.

In the middle of my work putting this anthology together, the most terrible tragedy imaginable occurred. On April 6, 2018, the Humboldt Broncos of the Saskatchewan Junior Hockey League, on their way by bus to a playoff game against the Nipawin Hawks, were involved in a horrendous accident that left 16 people dead (mostly teenage players plus two coaches, a driver, a broadcaster, a physiotherapist and a team statistician). Thirteen more were injured, many of those severely.

While there have been other tragic team bus accidents with fatalities, the scope of this catastrophe is unparalleled and has touched people all across Canada and indeed many other places in the world.

Saskatchewan was rocked by the blow that this awful tragedy inflicted on every citizen in the province. However, no matter the depth of the pain and the anguish, "the game of our lives" will continue on in every corner of the province. The Humboldt Broncos are already recruiting players for next season.

Finally, in putting this anthology together it was decided to concentrate on the grassroots of hockey in the fabric of the province. One could produce another volume that focuses on the province's contribution to the National Hockey League. To that end, Darrell Davis's essay at the end of the book is an amazing piece of writing that places the Saskatchewan NHL fraternity completely in the context of their roots in their home province.

It is fitting that the statue of Gordie Howe, "Mr. Hockey," graces page 3 in this anthology. If there is one individual whose life in hockey personifies the skill, toughness, honesty, humbleness and class that represents the spirit of Saskatchewan, it is the man who is arguably the game's greatest player.

— Allan Safarik
Dundurn, SK
2018

## Old Hockey Skates
*Glen Sorestad*

A rural kid, I honed my skating
and my hockey skills, such as they were
on a farm dugout which we scraped
shoved and shovelled clear of snowdrifts
before we could play a hockey game
without painted lines, without periods,
penalties or time clocks,
a game that might last all Sunday afternoon;

though bitter cold would force us to submit
when we could no longer feel our feet,
encased in battered second-hand skates,
then we would endure the agony
of thawing frostbitten toes in the warmth
of the farmhouse, whimpering with pain
as our feet whinged at how foolish we'd been.

I thought of this each time I watched
one or another of my grandsons
lace up his pair of pro-style hockey skates
in the warmth of the arena dressing room
before stepping onto that perfect
glistening sheet of freshly flooded ice,
not at all concave as a sway-backed nag,
the way our ice slumped in on itself
with the tiredness of January.

# Hockey Night

*Robert Currie*

I like to remember the outdoor rink, boards
that kept the puck out of snowbanks, prairie sky
full of stars almost as bright as the rink lights,
night air fresh and white with our breath,
pickup games, and we all took a turn in goal.
Always we played till our feet were numb,

then made for the shack, roaring wood stove
surrounded by benches where we sprawled,
our feet thrust at the stove and beginning
to throb with life, our bones warming till the smell
of our socks drove us back to the ice.

Then the repeated thrills, breaking for a goal, a pass
on your stick, the deke, the shot, puck in the net.
Transformed by ice and the night, Jari
Kurri and Paul Coffey beside me, I was
Wayne Gretzky veering behind the net.

I want to remember the way it was when sleep
would arrive as my head struck the pillow,
before my stomach was a burning knot,
my jaw sore, hands aching. A quarry of pain.
I try not to think of the game tonight, the moment
that always comes, when Coach says, "Come on,
big guy, time to earn your keep," when I throw
off my gloves and fight the other enforcer.

# Hockey Nights in Canada
## *Mansel Robinson*

I had a twin brother for a while. He's gone now. He became somebody he wasn't supposed to be. We were born with the same face, then he took that face and put it where it didn't belong.

We grew up in a small town that only has one band. They used to play at the legion hall about once a year. They learned a new song once a decade. They called themselves The Rhythm Renegades. We called them The Frozen Five. I guess making music is hard. I don't know. I never tried. My brother never tried either. He only ever tried one thing. But in that one thing he was a magician. He'd set himself up for a rebound like he could read the future. He could stickhandle so slick you never saw the puck till the red light blinked. No other word for it. Magician.

His name was Corky. Pretty good name, I guess. It's got a bit of something to it, and it coulda been famous, like Boom Boom or Toe. One time when we were about six, we were playing hockey in the street. Corky lifted a slapshot up about three feet and caught me right in the head. It left a perfect half-circle scar right over the eyebrows. Next year when we joined minor hockey, they stuck me in nets. They called me the bull's-eye. That's the name I go by even these days. I don't know what name Corky goes by these days. Maybe he gave that up too. I don't know.

I just wanted to skate. That's what I loved. One strange winter it hardly snowed at all. The wind kept the river swept clean for maybe a month. I'd skate for a mile or so, east and west; I knew the river better that winter than the ducks knew it in the summer. But I joined hockey and the coach went and stuck me in nets — he put me in the cage. I didn't really love the game, didn't really love it at all. Only wanted to skate. To me, that was like walking on water. Like racing against a white-tailed deer. Like dancing. But goalies don't dance. They wait. They called me Bull's-eye for a reason.

Twins, they said. But Corky had the magic wrists and I barely learned to juggle. I was okay as a goalie, but nothing even close to special. I took my

20 turns around the ice during warm-ups, then took my place at the end of the bench.

I got my skating done in other ways. Friday nights I'd go down to the rink, the same 10 scratchy records going round and round like the skaters. Then after hockey was finished for me, I got a job at the rink. A few guys were paid to clean the ice between periods and after the games. We just laced up our skates and pushed the snow off the ice with shovels. We skated round and round with our shovels like little machines. They have real machines now. Zambonis. They called us rink rats.

I played even after I was too old for minor hockey. Something to do. Monday nights a few of us would rent the rink — we got it cheap because I worked there. We had a jug of vodka and orange juice in the penalty box. You shoulda seen the lineup of guys wanting to get a penalty. My brother was playing junior by this time but he used to drop by once in a while to check us out. He called us The Monday Night Misfits.

You know what I wanted? I wanted to dance on the ice. I wanted to be a figure skater. But you didn't say that too loud around here. Those boys who wore the figure skates were accidentally on purpose made to feel unwelcome — they kinda drifted out of town one by one. I wanted to dance. And I never did. I loved to watch the figure skaters, though. Dancing on water.

Corky. He had a one-way ticket out of town — one way to the top. Money. Girlfriends. Whatever he wanted. He gave it up when he was 19. I don't know why. He just stopped. Cold. He had all that magic and he laughed at it. That son of a gun did nothing but watch it disappear.

Every once in a while somebody asks me why I never moved from here, never left home. I find that a funny question somehow. I would never ask somebody, Why do you believe in God? You either do or you don't. I don't see what there is to mess with. But sometimes when somebody asks me, I give an answer anyways. I tell them this: one time when I went to Hearst with the team. I was doing my job — bench-warming, riding the pine. A backup in case the starting goalie skated off the face of the earth.

We stayed at the hotel and we all stayed up late, talking about the sex we were going to have someday and having water fights in the meantime.

The coach finally got everybody settled down and the hotel was quiet. It was about 3 in the morning. I wasn't sleepy so I was standing looking out the window. I saw a woman come walking down the street by herself. She was right in front of my window when a guy on an old Ski-Doo stopped beside her. They talked for a bit. I thought maybe they were friends. Then he grabbed her and threw her on the seat of the Ski-Doo. Then he sat on her and drove it down the street. Right past the police station. She was screaming. And then it was quiet again.

Sometimes I tell people that's why I never left this town. Sometimes they understand.

I don't know why Corky threw his magic away. Maybe it came too easy for him.

Or maybe it wasn't even me who saw that woman and the Ski-Doo. Maybe it was him standing at the window, unable to move.

## Anecdote of the Hockey Game
### *Gerald Hill*

When a twelve-year-old boy, early for his ice time,
enters Dressing Room 8, picks a spot
to dump his equipment and sit down
while the old-timers pack up and leave,
a man named Roger, number 27, a man from Saskatchewan,
takes the opportunity to speak to the boy. *I'll tell you
a few things, he says. Listen.*

Out on the ice the kid plays quieter than usual,
Can't get him to say a single word, can't see
where he is. Sometimes you hear
his skates, behind, then ahead. The kid
skates for miles, doesn't mind darkness
or light, doesn't mind what gets in his way,
the masked faces, the red and blue lines.
He never gets where he's going but is always there,
looking for the loose puck, driving it home.

Toward the end of the third period with the game at its darkest,
he breaks across the blue line, no one
from him to the goalie, infinite time
to settle inside his next few moves. He breaks
in alone and lights up the red light just like
the man from Saskatchewan told him.

# Breakaway
*Maureen Ulrich*

In hockey there are so many variables. Twelve players on the ice at any given moment. Every one of them the key performers in her own little universe. Countless variations.

My boyfriend broke up with me.
My dad says I suck.
Why did I have to have my period *today*?
Then there's officiating.
A call—or a no call—can destroy a team's momentum in a second.

★★★

Too many variables.

In our second game against Saskatoon, all the planets roll and lock into perfect alignment. The fickle deities of ice hockey, suspended high above the play in their invisible luxury boxes, pluck the crucial weight from our golden plate and watch us rise.

Okay, hockey gods be damned.
Amy has a *lot* to do with it.

★★★

I have doubts about where I'll be playing one year from now. But there's no question about Amy Fox. She is destined for bigger things.

Then again, there's nobody like Bud to help put stuff in perspective.

"Do the math, girls," Bud says. "Saskatoon scored five power-play goals yesterday. Five-on-five you beat them one-zip. Stay out of the box, execute the PK properly when you don't, and play like you played yesterday. Show them you belong in this league."

We hit the ice running in the first period. We take it to the Stars on our very first shift, crashing the net and tallying four shots before their goalie finally freezes the puck. The momentum of the first line buoys the second.

Three minutes pass and the Stars still haven't moved the puck past their blue line. While we've got them tied up, our third line switches in, player by player.

Totally textbook.

Sue juggles the D too, throwing Carla and me back out.

One of the Stars cross-checks Larissa in front of the crease, and the ref raises her arm. Amy races for the bench while Randi barrels into the high slot as the sixth attacker. She hammers her stick, calling for the puck, and I saucer it over to her. Tape to tape.

She shoots. Low glove side. Buries it.

You'd think we'd won the Stanley Cup final instead of scoring the first goal against the second-ranked team in our league, the team that won the Mac's last December.

I'm on Randi's heels as we sweep by our shrieking bench. Sue nearly clotheslines me, yanking on my jersey and tugging me close. "Line up as a left-winger!" she shouts in my ear. "Randi's lining up on left D. Kathy's going to win the draw back to Randi. Give-and-go with Randi and she goes wide!"

I know Sue well enough not to question why.

★★★

When the linesman drops the puck, Kathy executes perfectly. As number 10 steps around me to cut Randi off, Randi snaps me the puck and I flip it back. The Stars' right D catches an edge trying to backpedal and Randi blows by her. We're three-on-one. The Stars' left D flops down to take away the back-door pass, but Randi rifles the puck to me

I wait. Wait for the goalie to move. Pull the trigger—going five-hole.

Red light.

I don't know what makes us happier—the fact we scored *again* or the fact we accomplished one of Sue's plays.

And Sue, the coach who rarely smiles, is grinning like a lion that's just swallowed the lion tamer, whip and all.

Bud squeezes my shoulder as I line up on the bench. "Great job, Cap," he murmurs in my ear. "No mercy now. Keep your foot on the gas."

# In Plain Sight
*William Robertson*

"[Shakespeare] saw, indeed, as I think, in Richard II the defeat that awaits all, whether they be Artist or saint, who find themselves where men ask of them a rough energy and have nothing to give but some contemplative virtue, whether lyrical phantasy, or sweetness of temper, or dreamy dignity, or love of God, or love of His creatures."
—Yeats on Richard II

It was hockey he wanted
and hockey he got
standing along the boards where
the players trooped out
him, his buddies, local experts all
watching their boys go forth
to be men, blades flashing
sticks cracking blood
of the fight

I watched from the stands
with other boys cut
or unable to play, we rejoiced
in the wins, ached with defeat, imagining ourselves heroes
to the girls among us

My father watched the boy
who would be his son-
in-law power up the ice
take the shot score the goal
pump the fist pretend to ignore
my father's righteous praise

While I lurked in plain sight
the fantastic warrior greedily
composing hymns to the infinite
of my abilities, the lion in repose
waiting to inherit my strength
waiting, in plain sight, where
my father tried, really tried,
to see me.

# My First Hockey Service
## Mick Burrs

I feel like an alien from a desert planet where no one skates, where ice is a mirage, and where the closest thing to pucks are camel droppings. It's my first live hockey game in Canada. Or should I say my first hockey service.

Here I am, sitting on one of the green benches in the bleachers near centre ice under a heater that isn't working, frigid air rising from the cement floor into the soles of my boots. I'm a visitor at the Al Ritchie Memorial Arena in Regina, Saskatchewan. And this is a late-night clashing the day after Christmas, 1980.

I huddle among hockey parents, secular worshippers in their community sanctuary. They've come to watch their cherubs in uniform play in the bantam league, the Cougars versus the Lions.

But I'll soon be given reason to believe that it's really the Christians versus the Lions, because tonight is the night I'll discover: hockey is not exactly in the same league as Sunday school.

On the bench in front of me, a hockey mother makes a verbal appeal for divine intervention. KNOCK HIS GODDAMN BLOCK OFF! ICE THE FUCKING THING!

So help me, she's got a babe against her breast and—WHERE TH' HELL DIDJA LEARN TA PLAY THIS GAME, YA FUCKING CHRYSANTHEMUM!

This modern madonna, Our Hockey Mother of the Curses, is chewing a wad of gum and holding an unlit cigarette in her free hand. Beautiful.

Another hockey mom is sitting beside me. She hardly says anything, watches silently, one could even say morosely.

Who is enjoying this service anyway?

The young players all look grim and determined, as if they were taking a mathematics exam. Their coaches resemble men who have just lost their jobs and are facing divorce, bankruptcy and a fatal disease all in one swoop.

And the adults in this congregation don't exactly sit there clapping their hands, smiling and laughing, looking serene.

Between the first and second periods, nearly everyone leaves the bleachers to get a shot of coffee in a Styrofoam cup or to smoke a cigarette, but this is bantam hockey, no fights, no violence. Not like what I see on television where the heroes of these young guys are all gods who use their sticks and their gloves and their flashing skates to express something other than brotherly love.

To make sure, however, that I don't leave this place with any wrong impressions about hockey's holy appeal and the primary expectations of its devoted worshippers, I watch some older kid not wearing a uniform walk onto the ice immediately after the service is over.

He punches a player in the face.

Hey, it's Boxing Day. Against all ritual, the losing team is instructed not to shake the winning team's hands.

Having achieved the proper spirit of this earthly religion, I frown as I walk out. I feel like I'm leaving a funeral parlour.

I have no illusions. I know this is a sacred sport played and watched in every city and village in Canada. It has winners and losers who all pray fervently for grace and violence and victory. But now you can see why I am also assured: they don't play hockey in heaven.

## At the Arena
*Kelley Jo Burke*

There is
fluorescence
stale popcorn
wood scarred by skate blades healed by falling beer
it's so ugly and cold and
familiar

the guys
horning their lust and rage
offer smokes to the snow maidens
cold-eyed at seventeen
who smile hiding their teeth
and turn back to the game

screams cut the Lutheran air

when everyone leaves
even the Zamboni man
when the unforgiving lights are finally down
and the ice is again virginal

skate out in the vaulting
dark

race and turn
like the great ones
the rafters reverberate with
your name
unassisted

the scoreboard shows
that Home has finally won

# Autumn 1972
## Randy Lundy

On Thursday, September 28, 1972, in Game 8 of what came to be known as the Summit Series, Team Canada tied the USSR—final score 5-5. After a tied first period, the Soviets outscored Canada 3-1 in the second and entered the third with a 5-3 lead. In the third, goals by Phil Esposito, his second of the night, and Yvan Cournoyer tied the game, but Canada couldn't manage the go-ahead goal, despite a flurry around the Soviet net in the final 30 seconds.

The series ended in a draw, with both teams sporting a record of 3-3-2. However, the Soviets claimed victory under international rules because they had outscored Canada 32-30 in the series. None of the Canadian players and no one in the entire country accepted this silly European statistical claim to victory, but nevertheless every Canadian, player and fan equally, was embarrassed and despondent.

It was not just a defeat on the ice surface but a national disgrace—to be beaten at our game and by the Russians. It was a victory for communism over the West and over democracy, and if they could beat us at hockey, what did they say about the possibility of their missiles outdoing those of our American protectors? Khrushchev was gone, but we would be subjected to Brezhnev, at every opportunity, reminding us of our failure.

It would come out in the press later that in the final minutes of play, the line of Phil Esposito, Yvan Cournoyer and Peter Mahovlich was supposed to come off for a line change. Bobby Clarke, Ron Ellis and Paul Henderson were supposed to have been on the ice in that final minute of the series. According to the interview Henderson gave the Toronto *Globe and Mail* after returning home, Pete Mahovlich had actually skated by the bench and while Henderson stood yelling for him to change, to get off the ice, Mahovlich had simply continued skating by.

"I had this strange feeling that I could score the winning goal," Henderson was quoted as saying, "but I never got the chance. I guess we'll never know."

In 1972 I was 10 years old, in fourth grade and living in a tiny, one-bedroom rented cabin in Flin Flon, Manitoba, with my father. Just the two of us, alone. My mother had left in the middle of July to visit friends in Thompson and had not returned. I wasn't too young to feel the impact of this, but it hadn't yet sunk in that she was not going to return. Ever. I am sure my father must have known. It wasn't unusual for her to leave for a few days or even a week and then return home—bleary-eyed, tired and volatile as a bear in a season with few berries—from what I now know must have been some hard partying. I knew the smell of whisky on her breath before I could name it.

I suppose when my father and I moved from our three-bedroom rented house to the smaller place, I should have clued in, but I was still young and untutored in the ways of the world, in the ways of relationships gone awry.

Dad worked 12-hour shifts underground in the zinc mine. A dirty business that left him exhausted. I was often with a babysitter. Eileen was a robust grey-haired widow who rented a cabin two doors down from us. Her husband had died in a shaft collapse. If it wasn't Eileen, then it was Jenny, a blond-haired 16-year-old whose bulging chest I couldn't get over. Girls in my grade didn't have breasts yet, and I found Jenny's endlessly fascinating, especially after the time she caught me staring and jokingly asked if I wanted to see them. I think she was joking but, mortally embarrassed, I didn't want to stick around to find out. I dashed out the door and headed for the maple tree I liked to climb to while away the hours. I would climb up 10 or 15 feet, sit on a branch to see what I could see, like the trout stream just beyond the oval collection of cabins. I would make up stories that made little sense. That afternoon I spun tales of what it would have been like, what might have happened if I had stuck around in the cabin with Jenny.

Flin Flon, Manitoba. Population 9,344, down from its peak in the early '60s, its heyday when the mining industry was booming. Between 1961 and 1971 the largest single-decade population decline occurred, but the population would continue to fall for the next 40 years. In another 40 maybe the place will be completely shuttered and abandoned.

Flin Flon, Manitoba, the birthplace and junior hockey home to both Reggie Leach, Reg 'The Rifle' Leach, and that great Stanley Cup leader, Bobby Clarke, who would lead the Philadelphia Flyers, the Broad Street Bullies, to consecutive Cup wins in 1974 and 1975. The same Bob Clarke who was supposed to be on the ice in the final minute of Game 8 versus the Russians.

My father and I watched the game together.

After the game, a commercial came on for a local furniture store that was having a *Team Canada Victory Sale Weekend* on Friday and Saturday. Sunday shopping was a taboo, like many others, that had yet to be breached. I don't know if the sale went ahead or not, but my father got up slowly, walked the short distance to the television and turned it off. He returned to his seat at the kitchen table, to his cup of coffee, and lit another home-rolled cigarette. Then he buried his face in his hands, and for a minute I thought he was crying—my 300-pound miner father. But he wasn't crying. I didn't see him cry that night or ever—not even after I heard him speaking with my mother on the black dial phone (that for some reason reminded me of a coffin) a couple of weeks later, and it was clear to me from hearing only half the conversation that she would never be back.

He switched off the television and, after a few moments of complete silence, which frightened me, he lifted his face from his hands and took a sip of coffee and a drag from his cigarette.

He looked at the signed and framed photo of Leach and Clarke smiling in Flin Flon Bombers sweaters, the only picture hanging on those barren, wood-veneer panelled walls, before he broke the silence by quietly saying, with an undertone of threat that left no room for misunderstanding, "I think it's time for you to go to bed."

He was due at the mine at 7 and I had school in the morning. Jenny would be by to keep an eye on me before he left, and we would walk together the half-mile to the elementary school, after which she would continue the three blocks to the high school.

I had never heard my father sound so tired, so *defeated*. Could a man who at my age had already lived through the dust bowl and depression of the '30s on a Saskatchewan homestead, who was close to my age when World War II had erupted and taken his father away and returned him a broken, drunken and violent man, my father who left home at 16 to work in a logging camp north of Prince Albert, and a man who had worked the past 15 years underground in the mine—could such a man be so defeated by a tie hockey game and the loss of a hockey series? A loss that wasn't even really a loss?

I fell asleep that night to Mac Davis singing *Baby Don't Get Hooked On Me* playing on the radio.

The next day at school, us boys spoke of nothing but Game 8 and what could have been, what might have been, what should have been.

My father and I never again spoke about the series, although we had spoken of little else, except the weather, for the entire month of September. In fact, we spoke less and less about anything in the coming months and years, especially after that last phone call from my mother, whose voice I wouldn't hear again for 20 years, a year after my father's heart exploded from the stress of having been permanently laid off from the mine, from too much coffee, from too many cigarettes, from the silence he clung to like a stick of dynamite, holding in everything in his life that was unbearable.

For weeks after that final game, I had a recurring dream: Pete Mahovlich skates by the bench, Paul Henderson bursts to his feet and calls Mahovlich off the ice. Mahovlich listens and takes the gate to the bench, while Phil Esposito and Yvan Cournoyer stay on. Henderson jumps onto the ice and rushes straight for the Russian net. The Russians slam the puck around the boards, but it is intercepted by Cournoyer. He misses Henderson with a pass, but two Russians mishandle the puck and it's on Esposito's stick. He fires it at Tretiak in the net. Save. Henderson gets up behind the net where he has fallen, skates out front, he's open and he grabs the rebound, fires it but is stopped.

With Tretiak down and out, Henderson gathers in his own rebound, and with 34 seconds left, Foster Hewitt shouts, "They score! Henderson has scored for Canada!"

In my dreams, there is even a photograph of "The Goal," a photograph that was to become famous, in which Henderson—smiling, open-mouthed, arms raised in triumph—is leaping into the arms of number 12, Yvan Cournoyer.

Canada wins the series. No one fears that the Russian missiles might be bigger and better than those of the Americans. During bomb drill, hiding under our desks at school, no one is cowering. We kids smile inwardly with a confidence secured by our victory on the ice. Everyone believes democracy is stronger and will eventually win the Cold War.

However, history cannot be undone—not world history, the history of a community or the history of a family, even if it is just a father and a son living together, alone. I know the dream was mere wish fulfilment, a compensation for the bitter disappointment of what really took place.

No one in Flin Flon, from that time to present day, remembers much about September of 1972. They don't remember the first episodes of *The New Price is Right*, *Fat Albert and the Cosby Kids*, *Maude*, *The Waltons*, *The Bob Newhart Show*, or *M*A*S*H*.

They don't remember Fischer and Spassky playing chess in the middle of the Atlantic, in Iceland. They don't remember the 37 dead in the Blue Bird Café in Montreal. They don't remember the Munich Massacre at the Olympics, or Israel's response, and the letter bombs in the mail, including one in Montreal. They don't remember India's move toward becoming the thaw in Sino-Japanese relations. They don't remember Nixon's Watergate shenanigans. They don't remember Ferdinand Marcos declaring martial law in the Philippines. They don't remember the F-86 Sabre crashing into a packed ice-cream shop in Sacramento. They don't even remember the sporting events of September 1972: Mark Spitz's seven gold medals; Muhammad Ali's bludgeoning of a 37-year-old Floyd Patterson; the first World Hockey Association exhibition game in Quebec City, which the Nordiques lost 4-1 to the New England Whalers; or Roberto Clemente's 3,000th major league hit before he died in that plane crash off Puerto Rico, while ferrying earthquake relief to Nicaragua.

These are events remembered by other people, in other places.

I have moved on to other things since that long ago Thursday evening in September 1972 in Flin Flon, Manitoba, and the silence that descended in that room after the click of the television knob and the slow fade-out of the screen.

I attended university to avoid the bush and the mines and all that came with that life. I am unmarried and have no children of my own (and I am not flattering myself by saying that I had opportunities for that kind of life). Most often my house is filled with silence, and I am comfortable in that silence. I still make up stories to amuse myself, just like I used to do as a 10-year-old, sitting in the afternoon branches of a maple tree. This evening I will telephone my mother, who lives in Snow Lake, Manitoba, with an angry gold miner. We will not talk about him. We will not talk about my father. We will not talk about the summer, or autumn, of 1972.

## Wreck League
*Stephen Scriver*

It ain't so bad really
a guy gets to stickhandle a lot
without some goon
crawlin' up your back
and when you score
the bench doesn't clear out
you just raise your arms
then skate back to the bench
kinda embarrassed

actually I never thought
I could enjoy the game
without lookin' up
at the scoreboard
or thinking about the standings

hell I can't believe
I could sit down for a beer
with the same guys
I was doin' my damn'dest
to smear all over the ice
a few years ago

ah no one comes to the games
much anyways
just a few wives
and the rink rats

but what the hell —
there's no heroes
in an empty rink

## The Shut Out
*Dolores Reimer*

"Get away from me, shithead!"
Fiona was trying to dipsy-doodle away from Bob. They had been playing street hockey since just after supper. The score was 10-10. The street light by Doug's house created an umbrella of light making the boundary of their playing area a circle. It was Fiona, Kenny and Doug against Phil, Bobby and Gary.

"Fiona, your mom's here," Phil said as he picked the puck off her stick. He dodged Kenny, stickhandling his way to where Gary stood with his goalie stick protecting a space between the two coffee cans filled with ice near the edge of the light circle.

Fiona turned to look. There she was. Navy parka unzipped, slippers on her feet, no gloves, and her arms moving up and down like crows' wings in summer. "Caw caw caw," thought Fiona, watching Jacqueline's mouth move up and down, not hearing the words. She took off her toque.

"Come here, Fiona, right this minute."

I could run ... straight down this street to the highway and on and on. She knew she was in trouble. She walked to her mother.

"Fiona Louise, that was no way for a lady to talk! I knew as soon as I saw you out here playing hockey again you'd be using strong language. A lady doesn't curse. Get in the house right now. You're too old to play with boys! Put that stick down and go finish your homework."

Fiona looked at Jacqueline. How did I ever end up with her as a mother, she wondered, looking at how green her skin appeared in the street light. She looked like an old Martian with her face screwed up in the *disapproval* look, her mouth coloured with Avon's Poppy Red lipstick. The white vapour from her hot breath hitting the outside air evaporated above her head the way cigarette smoke dissipated in air. Fiona watched as it floated above and disappeared against the dark sky. The sour smell of Jacqueline's breath wafted toward her.

"Phil," Fiona raised her voice. "Thanks for the stick."

"See you tomorrow, Fiona."

"Yeah, see you."

Fiona shoved the butt end into the snowbank and turned to follow her mother home. She heard the boys giggle and a falsetto "Ladies don't talk like that." Then more laughter. She had never felt so embarrassed in her life.

"Really, Fiona, girls don't play hockey and you shouldn't play with boys anymore. What are people like Mr. and Mrs. Baker going to think?" Jacqueline opened the door and let Fiona walk into the house before her.

"Mom, I was just playing hockey."

"But that will lead to other things and you'll get a reputation for being fast. Ladies don't hang around with boys and they don't talk the way I heard you speak out there. You're grounded for a week. No staying with Brenda on the weekend."

"Mom, that's not fair. There is nothing to do in the house in the winter." Fiona took off her parka and hung it in the closet, then put her mitts on the hot-air register so they would be dry in the morning.

"Fiona, shut your mouth and don't talk back. The boys won't have respect for you if you play hockey with them. In the end, when all is said and done, they won't treat you like a lady — they'll be too familiar and you won't have any mystique. Besides, I don't want you hanging around with that Phil. He's trouble, I hear." Her eyes narrowed. "What else has been happening out there?"

"Nothing."

"I hope none of them have tried to kiss you."

"Mom! We just play hockey."

"No more. I forbid you to play. No daughter of mine is going to hang around boys and ruin her reputation. Now get to your room. I don't want to see you anymore tonight. And don't forget, you're grounded."

The next morning it was still dark when Fiona walked to the bus stop. Kenny, Bobby, Phil and Doug were huddled in a circle smoking.

"Fiona," Phil said and nodded.

"Did you catch shit last night?" Kenny asked.

"A bit," she said. "Look, I'm really sorry. But, uh, is the big game against George and his gang still on for Sunday night?"

"THE BUS IS COMING! THE BUS IS COMING!" Bobby's little brother David yelled. The boys dropped their smokes and passed around a pack of Wrigley's Doublemint before Mr. Butcher could catch them smoking.

"Uh, yeah," said Doug, looking at the ground. "But we don't want you to play anymore. Your mom makes trouble for us with our folks. Sorry."

"You're good for a girl," Kenny said. "And maybe we need another player, but we can't have your mom stopping the game on Sunday."

Fiona could hardly see the steps of the bus when she climbed aboard. She felt foolish with her eyes full of tears. Blindly she found her friend Brenda, who always saved her a seat.

"You're lucky to have the same bus stop as Phil. He's so cute. Can you come to my house and do homework tonight?"

"No, I'm grounded."

"What did you do?"

"Nothing. Just played hockey. I think she heard me swearing."

"Mothers are B-I-T-C-H-es," Brenda said. "Look at the ugly pants mine made me wear."

Fiona pressed the tip of her index finger on the frosty bus window and watched as a clear space melted. She blew on it until it was large enough to look out and watched the trees and buildings go by. She looked out the window, making her peephole bigger and bigger while the schoolgirls sang their repertoire of Petula Clark's Downtown; Found a Peanut; Diana Ross; and Nancy Sinatra.

Fiona sang quietly along with them.

> "These boots are made for walking
> And that's just what they'll do
> One of these days, these boots are gonna
> Walk all over you."

Fiona thought this was a funny song. On the Ed Sullivan Show, Nancy Sinatra was wearing white go-go boots and everyone on the bus was wearing brown or black snow boots. She pictured snow boots possessed by the Devil walking by themselves over people.

"Brenda, do you ever feel like running away?" Fiona turned away from the window.

"Yeah, when my mom's a real bitch and it seems like I can't do anything right."

The bus pulled up to Scott Junior High.

"See you after school," Brenda said as they climbed off the bus.

Fiona stood where the bus left them and watched as Phil and the boys and Brenda and the rest of the kids walked into the school. She looked down the road. I could just walk and walk and walk and keep going forever. No one would miss me. She looked across the street at the arena. "Girls don't play hockey. It's unladylike to sweat," She mimicked. "Ladies wear dresses, why do you want to wear those pants? Keep your knees together..." The buzzer rang. She turned and ran for the front doors of the school.

★★★

"Hey Dad, wouldn't it be great to play in the NHL?"

Fiona and Peter were making popcorn. It was Saturday night. Hockey Night in Canada was on TV. Peter was pouring melted butter over the bowl of popped corn.

"It's nice to know I have a date every Saturday night in the winter." Peter winked at her.

Fiona just grinned and handed Peter his rye and coke. She took a sip of her orange juice.

"Where's the rooster?" he asked.

"Who?"

"The rooster ... your mother."

Fiona stared, puzzled, at Peter.

"Don't you think she reminds you of a rooster in the morning with her hair standing on end and all that crowing?"

"Not with that hair."

Peter downed half his drink and topped it up with rye.

"Come on, let's go watch the game. Boston and Toronto, my girl."
"Boston's my favourite team." Fiona sat on the floor in front of the television.
"Is Bobby Orr your favourite hockey player?"
"No. Derek Sanderson."
"Aahh, he's a goon."
"Oh Dad! He's real cute, and when he skates, his hair blows behind him. Brenda thinks he's cute too. Shelly likes Bobby Orr, but Brenda and I think he's too baby-faced."
"Peter, really, you shouldn't be encouraging her about this hockey business." Where did the mother come from?
"Hey Jackie, what's the big deal? A lot of women like hockey."
"She wants to play.
"It's impossible for girls to play, so don't worry about it. Leave the girl alone. There's no harm done."
"YES! Cheevers stopped him." Fiona cheered.
"Fiona! Don't yell in the house." Jacqueline spoke firmly as she zipped up her jacket.
"Say hello to Joyce for me. Look at him move! Baby face or not, Fiona, you're looking at history."
"Oh, for heaven's sake, I'll be home when I'm home."
Both Fiona and Peter erupted in cheers.
"One-nothing for us, Dad."
Fiona heard her mother close the outside door.
"Hey Dad, wouldn't it be great to play in the NHL? Heck, I'd be happy just to play hockey here in Memorial arena. I love the sounds and the smell of the ice."
"Girls can't play hockey," Peter said gently. "Street hockey is one thing, forget about the arena."
"I wish I were a boy," Fiona said quietly.
"Come now, I don't," Peter said.
"But then you wouldn't tell me to hush and not think about it when I tell you how hard I imagine what it feels like skating fast down the ice, hair blowing behind and Foster Hewitt saying, 'He's split the defense.

He shoots; he scores. What a fine play, ladies and gentlemen!' Why is it wrong to imagine?"

"Give it up, princess; it won't get you anywhere. Pay attention to the game now."

★★★

Fiona opened her eyes and stared at the ceiling. She heard the Bakers' car start. Fiona looked at her alarm clock. Ten o'clock, must be time for church. Sunday. Fiona felt knife-like stabs in her stomach. The day of the big game and she couldn't play. She rolled on her stomach, burying her face in the pillow hoping she could go back to sleep and wake up on Monday, hockey game over, and she wouldn't even ask who won.

"Fiona, don't be a lazy bones; get out of bed," Jacqueline called just outside her door.

"In a minute," she answered.

Fiona rolled herself deeper in her blankets, knowing her feet would get cold as soon as she stepped out of bed. She heard the telephone ring.

"Fiona, it's for you."

"Coming." She got up and ran to the kitchen.

"It's Brenda."

"Hello."

"Fiona, Gary wants to talk with you; he's here … the guys thought your mom wouldn't let you talk if they phoned, so hang on a minute."

"Okay."

"Uh, Fiona?"

"Yeah."

"Is your mom listening?"

"Yeah."

"Just answer yes or no then. We guys thought, you know, like, since this was such a big game and everything, that we should make it real and have a ref. So we took a vote and even George figured, like, you'd be the best person. Maybe if you're just, you know, reffing, your mom wouldn't get so mad, hey. So what do you think?"

"Uh, I don't know."

"C'mon Fiona, it's important; you know that."

"Oh, all right ... but it's not what I want to do."

"Good, I'll tell Phil."

Sunday was cold all day. Fiona finished the Sunday dinner dishes. She put her coat and boots near the door. Jacqueline was playing her usual game of solitaire in the living room. Peter was snoring. The Kraft man was giving a recipe on TV. Fiona put on her coat and as she closed the door on the warmth of the house, she could hear the slap slap of Jacqueline's cards and the Kraft man's voice as smooth as the peanut butter he was proclaiming.

Silence. She could hear the slight hum of the electrical meter. She walked down the driveway to the street, snow squeaking under her boots. She saw the guys down the road standing in a group. Waiting for her. This was the showdown.

"Fiona." Phil nodded to her and stepped on his cigarette.

"Okay, let's go," George said.

Gary paced out the perimeter of the rink, staying within the area of the street lamp.

"You know the rules," Phil said to the guys and handed Fiona the puck. "All we need you for is faceoffs and running after the puck if it goes out of bounds. We only have two tonight so keep an eye on them."

"Okay." Fiona walked to the centre of the rink. Bobby and Wayne were picked to take the faceoff. Fiona dropped the puck and the game was underway.

Phil had the first chance to score but put a wrist shot just wide of the jam cans. Fiona had run all the way to the Greens' house two doors away to retrieve the puck. He had another chance after the next faceoff, but Raymond caught the puck in his baseball glove. George won the next faceoff and Fiona had to hex him real hard to make sure he missed his chance. Doug deflected the puck to the Ridings' garbage can. It landed in a snowbank. They stopped the game to look for the puck. No one could find it. George reached into his coat pocket and brought out the other puck.

"Intermission between periods," Phil said.

The play went back and forth with no one scoring. Fiona kept wishing she could play instead of Kenny. She was better than him. And she could see that Raymond was weak on his left side. "Low and to the left, I could score on him," she thought as she ran to get the puck. As she brought it back to the guys, she heard them talking in the distance.

"Great to have your own little groupie," said George.

"Yeah. Comes in handy when you need someone to get the puck. She'll do anything for us."

"Anything, Phil?"

Phil only smiled back.

As Fiona handed the puck back to Phil, she felt anger start to burn in her. How could they! She was a hockey player, not a groupie. What was going on?

Bobby misdirected a shot past her feet. It hit the snowbank and careened all the way to her house. She just stood and watched it.

"Hey! Fiona!" The guys started yelling.

She watched them carefully, was going to refuse. Just then she heard Jacqueline's voice yelling in the distance.

"Fiona? FIONA!"

She started running toward her house.

"Aw jeez, it's her mother," she heard someone say as she reached the puck and picked it up.

"Here, go see your mother; I'll take it from here," Phil said as he caught up to her.

Fiona silently looked him straight in the eyes, then turned and kept running down the street.

"Hey!" Phil called. "Fiona, get back here."

"Fiona Louise!" she heard her mother's shrill yell behind her.

As she ran, her parka hood fell off her head. Fiona ran faster and faster. She was breathing great gulps of cold air. She ran as fast as she could. With her hood down, all she could hear was the roar of the wind in her ears. This is what hockey players hear. She thought of the roar of the crowd on Hockey Night in Canada. This is what they hear skating down the ice. She clutched the puck harder in her hand. She knew Phil was behind her; she ran faster and faster to the end of the street to the baseball field. There was nothing but snow covering it; no one had walked on the field in months. When she reached the edge, Fiona twirled like a discus thrower—once, twice, three times around.

"A spin-a-rama. SHE SHOOTS; SHE SCORES!" Fiona yelled as she let go of the puck and watched it arc into the dark winter night.

# Once Is Once Too Many
### *Stephen Scriver*

I only forgot to wear my can
once    that was enough
it was one time over in Glenavon
I went out for my first shift
and you know how when you're waiting
for the drop of the puck
you lean over and rest
your stick across your can
well, this time all I can feel
is wide-open spaces and the family jewels

but I'm not gonna skate
back to the bench
so I figger I'll get by
for the shift anyways

well; I'm all over the ice
like a mad man's shit and
I chase the puck into their corner
pass it back to Brian on defence
Then head for the net to screen the goalie

When I look back to the point
Sure as God's got sandals
Brian's just blasted one crotch-high

Not to worry I figger
I'll just jump and let it cruise
between my legs

well, I couldn'ta timed'er
more perfect      it was just
like a three-ball combination

'cept that two of them were damn
near in my throat
while the puck caroms into the net
like snot off a doorknob

was I pleased?
Is the Pope married?

# Goalie
*Rudy Thauberger*

Nothing pleases him. Win or lose, he comes home angry, dragging his equipment bag up the driveway, sullen eyes staring down, seeing nothing, refusing to see. He throws the bag against the door. You hear him fumbling with his keys, his hands sore, swollen and cold. He drops the keys. He kicks the door. You open it and he enters, glaring, not at you, not at the keys, but at everything, the bag, the walls, the house, the air, the sky.

His clothes are heavy with sweat. There are spots of blood on his jersey and on his pads. He moves past you, wordless, pulling his equipment inside, into the laundry room and then into the garage. You listen to him, tearing the equipment from the bag, throwing it. You hear the thump of heavy leather, the clatter of plastic, the heavy whisper of damp cloth. He leaves and you enter. The equipment is everywhere, scattered, draped over chairs, hung on hooks, thrown on the floor.

You imagine him on the ice: compact, alert, impossibly agile and quick. Then you stare at the equipment: helmet and throat protector, hockey pants, jersey, chest and arm protectors, athletic supporter, knee pads and leg pads, blocker, catching glove and skates. In the centre of the floor are three sticks, scattered, their broad blades chipped and worn. The clutter is deliberate, perhaps even necessary. His room is the same, pure chaos, clothes and magazines everywhere, spilling out of dresser drawers, into the closet. He says he knows where everything is. You imagine him on the ice, focused, intense, single-minded. You understand the need for clutter.

When he isn't playing, he hates the equipment. It's heavy and awkward and bulky. It smells. He avoids it, scorns it. It disgusts him. Before a game, he gathers it together on the floor and stares at it. He lays each piece out carefully, obsessively, growling and snarling at anyone who comes too close. His mother calls him a gladiator, a bullfighter. But you know the truth, that gathering the equipment is a ritual of hatred, that every piece represents, to him, a particular variety of pain.

There are black marks scattered on the white plastic of his skates. He treats them like scars, reminders of pain. His glove hand is always swollen. His chest, his knees and his biceps are always bruised. After a hard game, he can barely move. "Do you enjoy it?" you ask. "Do you enjoy the game, at least? Do you like playing?" He shrugs. "I love it," he says.

Without the game, he's miserable. He spends his summers restless and morose, skating every morning, lifting weights at night. He juggles absent-mindedly —tennis balls, coins, apples —tossing them behind his back and under his leg, see-sawing two in one hand as he talks on the phone, bouncing them off walls and knees and feet. He plays golf and tennis with great fervour, but you suspect, underneath, he is indifferent to these games.

As fall approaches, you begin to find him in the basement, cleaning his skates, oiling his glove, taping his sticks. His hands move with precision and care. You sit with him and talk. He tells you stories. This save. That goal. Funny stories. He laughs. The funniest stories are about failure: the goal scored from centre ice, the goal scored on him by his own defenceman, the goal scored through a shattered stick. There is always a moral, the same moral every time. "You try your best and you lose."

He starts wearing the leg pads in September. Every evening, he wanders the house in them, wearing them with shorts and a T-shirt. He hops in them, does leg lifts and jumping jacks. He takes them off and sits on them, folding them into a squat pile to limber them up. He starts to shoot a tennis ball against the fence with his stick.

As practice begins, he comes home overwhelmed by despair. His skill is an illusion, a lie, a magic trick. Nothing you say reassures him. You're his father. Your praise is empty, invalid.

The injuries begin. Bruises. Sprains. His body betrays him. Too slow. Too clumsy. His ankles are weak, buckling under him. His muscles cramp. His nose bleeds. A nerve in his chest begins to knot and fray. No one understands. They believe he's invulnerable, the fans, his teammates. They stare at him blankly while he lies on the ice, white-blind, paralyzed, as his knee or his toe or his hand or his chest or his throat burns.

To be a goalie, you realize, is to be an adult too soon, to have too soon an intimate understanding of the inevitability of pain and failure. In the backyard, next to the garbage, is an old garbage can filled with broken hockey sticks. The blades have shattered. The shafts are cracked. He keeps them all, adding a new one every two weeks. You imagine him, at the end of the season, burning them, purging his failure with a bonfire. But that doesn't happen. At the end of the season, he forgets them and you throw them away.

You watch him play. You sit in the stands with his mother, freezing, in an arena filled with echoes. He comes out without his helmet and stick, skating slowly around the rink. Others move around him deftly. He stares past them, disconnected, barely awake. They talk to him, call his name, hit his pads lightly with their sticks. He nods, smiles. You know he's had at least four cups of coffee. You've seen him, drinking, prowling the house frantically.

As the warm-up drills begin, he gets into the goal casually. Pucks fly over the ice, crashing into the boards, cluttering the net. He skates into the goal, pulling on his glove and blocker. He raps the posts with his stick. No one seems to notice, even when he starts deflecting shots. They come around to him slowly, firing easy shots at his pads. He scoops the pucks out of the net with his stick. He seems bored.

You shiver as you sit, watching him. You hardly speak. He ignores you. You think of the cost of his equipment. Sticks, $40. Glove, $120. Leg pads, $1,300. The pads have patches. The glove is soft, the leather eaten away by his sweat.

The game begins, casually, without ceremony. The scoreboard lights up. The ice is cleared of pucks. Whistles blow. After the stillness of the faceoff, you hardly notice the change, until you see him in goal, crouched over, staring.

You remember him in the backyard, six years old, standing in a ragged net wearing a parka and a baseball glove, holding an ordinary hockey stick, sawed off at the top. The puck is a tennis ball. The ice is cement. He falls down every time you shoot, ignoring the ball, trying to look like the goalies on TV. You score, even when you don't want to. He's too busy play-acting. He smiles, laughs, shouts.

You buy him a mask. He paints it. Yellow and black. Blue and white. Red and blue. It changes every month, as his heroes change. You make him a blocker out of cardboard and leg pads out of foam rubber. His mother makes him a chest protector. You play in the backyard, every evening, taking shot after shot, all winter.

It's hard to recall when you realize he's good. You come to a point where he starts to surprise you, snatching the ball out of the air with his glove, kicking it away with his shoe. You watch him one Saturday, playing with his friends. He humiliates them, stopping everything. They shout and curse. He comes in, frozen, tired and spellbound. "Did you see?" he says.

He learns to skate, moving off of the street and onto the ice. The pain begins. A shot to the shoulder paralyzes his arm for 10 minutes. You buy him pads, protectors, thinking it will stop the pain. He begins to lose. Game after game. Fast reflexes are no longer enough. He is suddenly alone, separate from you. Miserable. Nothing you say helps. Keep trying. Stop. Concentrate. Hold your stick blade flat on the ice.

He begins to practise. He begins to realize that he is alone. You can't help him. His mother can't help him. That part of his life detaches from you, becoming independent, free. You fool yourself, going to his games, cheering, believing you're being supportive, refusing to understand that here, in the rink, you're irrelevant. When you're happy for him, he's angry. When you're sad for him, he's indifferent. He begins to collect trophies.

You watch the game, fascinated. You try to see it through his eyes. You watch him. His head moves rhythmically. His stick sweeps the ice and chops at it. When the shots come, he stands frozen in a crouch. Position is everything, he tells you. He moves, the movement so swift it seems to strike you physically. How does he do it? How? You don't see the puck, only his movement. Save or goal, it's all the same.

You try to see the game through his eyes, aware of everything, constantly alert. It's not enough to follow the puck. The position of the puck is old news. The game. You try to understand the game. You fail.

He seems unearthly, moving to cut down the angle, chopping the puck with his stick. Nothing is wasted. You can almost feel his mind at work, watching, calculating. Where does it come from, you wonder, this strange mind? You try to move with him, watching his eyes through his cage, and his hands. You remember the way he watches the game on television, cross-legged, hands fluttering, eyes seeing everything.

Suddenly you succeed, or you think you do. Suddenly, you see the game, not as a series of events, but as a state, with every moment in time potentially a goal. Potentiality. Probability. These are words you think of afterwards. As you watch, there is only the game, pressing against you, soft now, then sharp, then rough, biting, shocking, burning, dull, cold. No players. Only forces, feelings, the white ice, the cold, the echo, all joined. A shot crashes into his helmet. He falls to his knees. You cry out.

He stands slowly, shaking his head, hacking the ice furiously with his stick. They scored. You never noticed. Seeing the game is not enough. Feeling it is not enough. He wants more, to understand completely, to control. You look out at the ice. The game is chaos again.

He comes home, angry, limping up the driveway, victorious. You watch him, dragging his bag, sticks in hand, leg pads over his shoulder. You wonder when it happened, when he became this sullen, driven young man. You hear the whispers about scouts, rumours. Everyone adores him, adores his skill. But when you see his stiff, swollen hands, when he walks slowly into the kitchen in the morning, every movement agony, you want to ask him why. Why does he do it? Why does he go on?

But you don't ask. Because you think you know the answer. You imagine him, looking at you and saying quietly, "What choice do I have? What else have I ever wanted to do?"

## Going Down

*Stephen Scriver*

Yer not playing with a full deck
if you go down to block a shot
in this kinda hockey—
take Dickie there   did it once too often
and hasn't laced on a skate since

It was the '72 playoffs
the Monarchs had a power play
and Latourneau winds up at the point
with a shot so hard
he damn near tears out his arsehole

Well. Dickie goes down to block
And for a second there's no puck
till he spits it out
right on the blue line
with about a dozen teeth

Latourneau?   Hell, he takes that puck
Stickhandles through them teeth and scores
While we stand there crotch-bound
like a buncha decoys

Dickie? Well, he never was much
to look at anyways.

## Stanislowski Vs. Grenfell
*Stephen Scriver*

It is noted
without metrics or mourning
that the world's foremost violinist
played in Grenfell
to the assembled chairs of the legion hall

while two-thirds of the populace
was attending a four-pointer
between the Spitfires and Whitewood
at the Community Recreation Centre

No surprise in a town where
There's more agriculture
Than culture, and Art
Is the guy who runs the Paterson elevator

# Indian Head, Saskatchewan
July 1997
*Bill Boyd*

Indian Head, between Yorkton and Regina, has fewer than 2,000 people, but its main street is called Grand Avenue and it is wider than the nearby Trans-Canada Highway. Along the street there's Bigway Foods, a Stedmans, two drugstores, the Sportsman's Pub and the office of the Economic Development and Tourism Committee. The opera house, built in the late 1800s, is now the Nite Hawk cinema but it has just changed hands and the new owners may renovate it for live entertainment. It's almost de rigueur for Prairie towns to have at least one Chinese restaurant, testimony to the indentured Chinese who built the railways, and Indian Head's is the China Garden. On the streets off Grand Avenue are big, stone houses, built by the Scots and English who came to farm a hundred years ago.

The *Indian Head-Wolseley News* comes out each Tuesday. According to its masthead it also covers the news in Qu'Appelle, Montmartre, Odessa and Carry the Kettle. "I try to be positive," says Ken McCabe, the publisher. "I don't go looking for a fight." McCabe, 60 years old, has spent most of his life in Indian Head. He left school after Grade 10, worked eventually as the town's recreation director and wrote sports for the newspaper. When local businessmen bought it to keep it out of the hands of out-of-towners, they asked McCabe to run it. "If we have bad weather and bad crops, I report it," he says. "But you can't go poor-mouthing everything and expect people to move here and do business. Agriculture is still the big thing here. We have the government experimental farm and a tree nursery. Not many small towns in Saskatchewan have as many trees as we have. This year alone we planted 3,200 at the golf course and we have new grass greens, a new swimming pool, and the rink's fairly new."

McCabe, with his glasses, greying moustache and greying hair, might pass for Jacques Demers, the coach of the Tampa Bay Lightning. McCabe played goal for years for the Indian Head Chiefs, a senior hockey team. Depending on which teams were operating, the Chiefs were in the Mainline League or the Triangle League or the Qu'Appelle Valley League. He was 14 or 15 when he played his first senior game. "I hitchhiked to Qu'Appelle, nine or 10 miles down the road, to see a game and one of the goalies didn't show up. I played for the Wolseley Mustangs against the Fort Qu'Appelle Sioux Indians and we lost 10-6. They paid me five bucks. Hockey was a big attraction back then and we got big crowds, six, seven hundred, not just Indian Head, but other towns, too. Winter was hockey or curling. That was it.

"Over the years we had some good hockey players, guys maybe just a couple steps short of making it up there. But the best we ever had was a fellow named Jerry Walker. He was a big scorer for the Regina Pats, and remember, they were one of the best junior teams in the whole goddamn country. The New York Rangers wanted him but instead he went to university in the States. He came here to work for the Royal Bank. I never played with anyone who could dominate a game the way he could."

The office of the *Indian Head-Wolseley News* is between a convenience store and the liquor store in the Arrowhead Mall, at the bottom of Grand Avenue, near the CPR line and the grain elevators. McCabe puts out the paper with the help of three women; two of them are his daughters. Sharing his office space is the Rural Sports Hall of Fame and Museum, which he created. There are Grey Cup programs from way back and baseball uniforms and football and hockey sweaters, and footballs and baseballs and bats, hockey sticks and curling brooms. There are golf clubs and boxing gloves and piles and piles of photos, some recent, some from before the First World War. McCabe is also one of those responsible for bringing athletes to town for sports dinners and such. "Henri Richard has been to Indian Head, and Guy Lafleur, Norm Ullman and Gilbert Perreault," McCabe says. "George Chuvalo, too, talking about drug abuse." He waves a finger for emphasis. "And I've done it without any government help. It's not worth having to do all sorts of goddamn paperwork just to satisfy some bureaucrats."

On the wall, there's a photo of Murray Westgate, the actor who for years did the Esso commercials for TV's *Hockey Night in Canada*. "He went to school here," McCabe says. There's also one of Eric Peterson, of TV's *Street Legal.* "He was born here. He comes back to see his mother." And there's a picture of Johnny Esaw, the longtime CTV sportscaster. McCabe says Esaw once broadcast baseball games from Indian Head.

He picks up a photograph album. "Look at these. In the '40s and '50s we hosted the biggest baseball tournaments in Western Canada. We'd draw fifteen, twenty thousand. The pictures are right here." And they are, showing thousands of people in the stands and ringing the field. McCabe goes on, "A lot of hockey players played ball here," and he goes to a stack of handwritten lineups that include the names Doug and Max Bentley, Bill Mosienko, Gordie Howe, Metro Prystai, Emile Francis, Bert Olmstead, Jackie McLeod, Nick and Don Metz, and Bill and Gus Kyle. Rollie Miles, the great Edmonton Eskimo, is there, too. "And look here." McCabe holds up two more photos. They're of Pumpsie Green, the first black to play for the Boston Red Sox, and Tom Alston, another black, who played parts of four seasons with the St. Louis Cardinals. "Lots of black kids played here in the summer. A team, the Jacksonville Eagles, used to come up from Florida and be the Indian Head Rockets for the season. When the Eagles stopped coming, their place was taken by the Florida Cubans."

McCabe's father walked out on the family when McCabe was three. "My mother and my sister and I lived in an apartment. My mother worked in a grocery store. She was very good, but if it hadn't been for the RCMP and my coaches and my teachers, and for sports, I don't know what would have happened to me. That's why I went ahead with the sports hall of fame, to give something back."

He goes on, "Maybe kids with single parents got special attention, but if we did, I needed it. We had a cop as football coach and he'd say, 'I know you were out drinking beer last night so if you want to be on this team, do 25 pushups,' things like that. Another time a baseball coach made me run all the way home for my baseball cap because he'd said practice was in full uniform and I'd forgotten it. I told him it wasn't important. He said if I wanted to play ball, it goddamn well was. And one night I came home late and the RCMP constable is parked right in front of the Windsor Apartments where we lived, right beside the livery barn.

He said, 'You come home late again and we're going into that barn and only one of us is coming out.' Can you imagine telling a kid that today? But it was what I needed."

Ken McCabe is quiet for a moment, sipping his Diet Coke. Then he says, "None of that seems very far back. I can still see a kid coming to the football field on horseback and tying that horse to a tree while he practised. And I'll never forget that before we had artificial ice around here, the rinks were so goddamn cold that being a goalie you nearly froze."

★★★

Not far from Indian Head, by the Qu'Appelle River, which keeps the Qu'Appelle Valley green in the summer and where generations of youngsters learned to skate in winter, Fred Brown has 2,500 acres under seed, and 80 head of cattle. Brown is 62, short, soft-spoken, with a farmer's hands and face. He played senior hockey with the Indian Head Chiefs from the age of 18 until he suffered a heart attack at 42. "It was the first game of the season and I got a butt end right here," he says, tapping the middle of his chest. "It hurt like hell but I figured I was just winded and I finished the game." The next morning, however, he nearly collapsed doing the milking. "Milking by hand," he says. "I went inside and told my wife that she better finish it for me and I went to lay down, and Jesus, I began to vomit and it hurt even worse so I figured then it was more than a butt end. She took me to the hospital."

Brown's playing days were finished, but that autumn he took over as coach, until his doctor read about it in the newspaper. "He gave me hell. He said there was far more stress coaching than playing, so I quit and started to play old-timers, and I still do."

Brown says that as a child he was a weak skater and the other kids made fun of him, so he quit. "When I was about 10, I started again and I skated until I learned how and I became a good skater. And it didn't matter whether it was 20 or 30 below, we cleaned the ice and played. There wasn't anything else to do then, no TV, no dope to smoke. I think it's harder on the kids today, there's so much going on."

The Regina Pats, a force in junior hockey, invited Brown to their training camp. "But it was September and we were still harvesting so I stayed on the farm. I've wondered sometimes if I should have gone, but I didn't so that's that. I played senior here for 24 years and I was captain for 18. How many people can say that? I'm really proud of it."

In his garage he has a seat from the old Montreal Forum. It cost him $340. He sits in it every day to pull his workboots on and off. "I've always been a Canadiens fan, which is rare around here. There's lots of Toronto and some Rangers and now Philadelphia. But the Canadiens, they're the great skaters and they know how to pass the puck and play position." He moves around in the old Forum seat, getting comfortable, and smiles. "Maybe my wife will let me bring it into the house when I watch them win their next Stanley Cup." Then he adds, "You know what I'd really like some day? I'd like to meet Jean Béliveau."

## Hockey Lesson
*Robert Currie*

Around the dugout
snow is piled.
Young Jacob stands
on ankles like spaghetti,
his blades pointing east and west
while Yarrow cuts another circle
on the dugout ice,
stickhandles like a rush
of Bentley brothers at a net.

Young Jacob watches,
lifts his stick and totters,
slams it, bangs it on the ice.
    I'm Teeder Kennedy, he calls.
    C'mon. Pass it here.
    I'm Teeder Kennedy.

Yarrow sweeps towards him,
lays a pass along the ice,
and just as Jacob reaches
picks it up again,
is gone while Jacob
turns with awkward, crooked steps
to watch him as he wheels
by and gone again.

Yarrow will teach him
who he is.

## Beneath the Frozen Moon
*Robert Currie*

Yarrow could forget the cold,
slashing shots at ankle height,
flicking rebounds back again,
Foster Hewitt shouting on the wind.
Inside he had the drive, the heat
to keep him warm.
He practised shots, stops,
invented ways to move
until the puck was just
another shadow on the ice.

Sitting on a log again
with brittle fingers he
untied, unlaced his skates,
pushed feet of stone into his boots,
set out across the moonlit field,
the wind tearing at his skin.

Before he was halfway home
he felt the moonlight in his feet,
the glow that danced between his toes,
the needled pain
that ran like a flame into his legs.
He didn't care.
Another day and he'd be playing
For the Leafs / he knew
there was witchcraft in his feet,
magic in the way he moved.
Beneath the frozen moon
he burned a path across the field.

# The Hockey Game
*Wes Fineday*

The knocking at my door woke me up. It was a Saturday morning, which meant that there was no school. I got out of bed, got dressed, then walked out of my bedroom and across the hallway to the bathroom. The door was closed. Someone was in there. I went back to the bedroom, made my bed, picked up my books and put them on the dresser. I had been doing my homework just before I fell asleep. There was still quite a bit to do.

Grade 9 sure wasn't easy, at least not as easy as Grade 8. I had finished my Grade 8 at boarding school last year. I had done quite well, in fact. This year was different. The Department of Indian Affairs had sent me to live in Moose Jaw to do my Grade 9. They explained to me that they had found me a good Christian boarding home to live in. They also told me that I should consider myself lucky to have this opportunity. At the time I wondered if it would be anything like the school I had left.

I went back to the bathroom. It was vacant. I had a good wash and went back to the bedroom.

They had driven me to Moose Jaw from the boarding school and with that move, everything changed. Now I was in a bedroom by myself instead of a dormitory with 30 other kids. The food eaten by these Christians was unlike anything I ever got at boarding school or at home. For breakfast they would eat dry cereal and pour milk over it to make it soggy. With this they ate toast that was also soggy with butter. For lunch and supper we would have meat and potatoes or rice. I'd eaten these before but not the way this woman cooked it. She used tomatoes and stuff that looked like powder that she kept in small jars above the stove. She must have had 20 different kinds of powder. It was awful. My stomach would hurt for hours after and sometimes I would get ill and bring it all up.

When I tried to tell her that I couldn't eat the food, she called me ungrateful and told me my parents would be glad to have something like this to eat. I doubted that. My parents liked eating rabbit and bannock, berries and potatoes just fine. But I didn't tell her that. Arguing would just get me into more trouble.

While I was eating breakfast, the woman who was my landlady explained to me that they were going on a family outing. "Not too many more nice weekends before the snow comes," she said. "We're going to take advantage of this one." I could hear the two little boys playing downstairs in the basement. They were playing with the electric train set their father had set up down there. I was not allowed to go near it. I was also not allowed to play with their two boys without permission. I wondered about that sometime. I did not understand why they treated me so differently from the way they treated everyone else. I suspected they did not like me. The landlady's voice intruded on my thoughts.

"Drink up your milk now and don't bother coming back until 9 o'clock this evening. The house will be locked."

These Christians sure didn't trust Indians, I thought, as I got up and took my dishes to the sink.

After breakfast I wandered outside to the backyard. The landlord was already out there washing his car. I sat on the back steps and watched him. "Come over here and give me a hand with this," he called. So I did. When we finished washing and waxing the car, he went back inside and soon they all came out. They seemed to be in a good mood, laughing and talking about the wild animal park. I got up and headed for the sidewalk and started walking down the street. I had nowhere to go, but I thought they would get mad if it looked like I was going to hang around the house all day. I was barely half a block from the house when they drove by. The parents were in front, looking straight ahead, the kids were sitting in the back, looking around. They waved as they went by. I waved back and smiled, trying to look happy.

I watched until the car turned the corner two blocks down the street, then I turned around and walked back to the house. I went into the backyard and stood on the back step for a while and finally sat down.

The backyard was separated from the yards on either side of it by a tall picket fence. There was also a garden at the back.

The neighbour's back door opened. A man and a woman followed by a little boy stepped outside. They did not see me. The man was dressed in shorts and a T-shirt, the woman in a bathing suit. They sat down on a couple of lawn chairs, which were placed around a small table. The little boy ran to the end of the yard, where there was a swing and a slide and a sandbox full of toys. I looked back at the parents. They had been joined by a small black dog with short curly hair. He was sprawled on the ground between the two people, soaking up the sun. I got up from the steps and went a little closer to the fence so I would be out of sight. I did not want them to think I was spying on them. They might get mad at me. From where I now sat, I could hear them talking about the new car they were planning to buy. The man talked about a contract for playing hockey. This meant they could get a new car. He also had another job. This would take care of their other bills.

I thought about my parents and family at home. My dad had more than two jobs. He had to catch horses before he could do anything. This was a job in itself. Our horses could run very fast and jump fences. Then he had to drive them out to the bush so he could chop wood and haul it home, where he sawed it into small pieces so it would fit in our cookstove. He also had to haul water. And hunt. He usually did this when he was out in the bush chopping wood. I could see him standing on top of a load of wood on the sleigh, or maybe walking beside it if it was really cold. It was better to keep moving on very cold days. There would usually be a rabbit or two and sometimes even three if he was lucky. We used to run outside to meet him and fight about who would carry the rabbits into the house to give to my mom. She was very good at cleaning and skinning rabbits. She had been doing it for years.

Too bad my dad couldn't get a job playing hockey, I thought. I was sure the folks back home who played hockey didn't get paid to do it. They just did it together to have fun. I had heard my dad telling a story to some people about a hockey game. They had cleared the ice on a section of the creek that runs through our reserve. A group of young fellows had got together to have a game. There were just about enough of them for two teams, but one of the teams was minus a goaltender. They managed to talk Leo, who didn't know how to skate, into putting on a pair of skates and being their goalie. Leo shoved some newspapers up each pant leg and wrapped them around his ankles and tied them with twine. Two of his teammates supported him on either side and pulled him out to his goal. He managed, barely, to stay on his feet by propping himself up with the crude goalie stick someone had hastily nailed together for him. For a puck, they were using a freshly frozen piece of horse dropping they had picked up in someone's barn. Dad said these really smarted if they hit an unprotected spot. The other boys had chopped down suitably curved willow trees for hockey sticks.

Leo's team won the game. Ecstatic over their victory, they all rushed off to the fire, which was roaring beside the creek. They didn't notice Leo until someone started laughing and pointing to the rink. There was Leo, crawling across the ice on hands and knees toward the fire, dragging his stick behind him.

I smiled remembering the story. Suddenly, I heard a car starting. I had forgotten about the people next door. While I had been thinking, or daydreaming, as my teachers called it, the neighbours had moved back inside. Now they had come back out and were about to drive off in their car. I looked up at the sun and realized I had been sitting there daydreaming all morning. And now I was hungry. Back home if you were hungry, you just went somewhere to visit at mealtime and you would be sure to get fed. I decided to give it a try. I tried to think of someone I could go visit. There was Allen, who lived across the street and was in my class at school. But he hadn't been very friendly to me. I decided not to go over there. A few houses down lived another kid who was in my class. His name was Robert. He asked me if I wanted to come to the fields beside their place and play football. I had wanted to but I didn't know how to play football, so I had declined the invitation.

I got up and walked down the street. When I reached their house I almost turned around but I was hungry. I thought it was a funny thing no one ever used their front door since it was closer to the street. They all used the back door. Our house at home only had one door so we had no choice. I stood there trying to muster the courage to knock on the door. The screen door was the only obstacle between me and the food. I could smell cooking inside. That spurred me on. I knocked and waited. I could hear voices and finally a very tall lady came to the door.

"Is Robert home?" I asked, hoping she would invite me in.

"Yes, he's in," she replied. "But he's having his dinner. Why don't you come back in half an hour or so? He should be finished by then." With that she closed the door and walked away. I felt embarrassed, thinking she must have known why I was there.

Well, I wouldn't try that again. I turned around and retraced my steps to the backyard of the house where I lived. It was then I noticed the carrots in the garden. Too dangerous, I decided; my landlady would notice if I took even one. I sat down by the fence and immediately fell asleep. I must have slept most of the afternoon, because when I awoke the neighbours were back. I could hear them talking on the other side of the fence. I got up and went over to the fence. There was an outside tap sticking out of the wall of the house. The landlady ran a hose from the garden to water those carrots. I thought of them again. My hunger had returned. It was more urgent now. I turned on the tap and let the water run over my arms and hands. It felt cool and refreshing. I cupped my hands and filled them up, stuck my face in the water and felt a tingle go all the way down to my toes. I was awake again. I dried myself off with my shirt sleeves. Then I went and sat back down in my spot. There I felt safe.

"Make mine kind of rare, I like it like that," said the woman. Suddenly I was blasted by the aroma of meat cooking over a fire. I knew the smell, having often eaten meat cooked over a fire. I was just drifting off on memories of home when the man next door yelled, "That damn dog!" Just then the dog came bounding around the corner of the fence and into the yard I was in. It was carrying a steak in its mouth. The man was not far behind. He came running around the fence, still carrying the huge fork he must have been using to turn the meat. So preoccupied with what was behind that it totally ignored anything in front of it, the dog ran right into me. The dog and the man came to a dead stop.

"Well, hello there. I didn't think there was anyone home here," the man said to me.

"There isn't," I answered. "They went somewhere for the day. They're not going to be home until around 9 o'clock."

"Do you live here?" he asked, seeming to have forgotten about the steak.

"Yes," I answered.

"Have you eaten yet?"

"No," I replied, not daring to look at the man.

"We were just going to eat. You could join us if you want to. Come on," he urged. I did not need much urging. He speared the steak the dog had dropped, turned around and started to walk back into his yard, his dog and me close behind.

I did not leave any of the huge steak they served me. I could barely move, but I somehow managed to put away a large helping of ice cream for dessert. It was the best meal I had eaten in a long time.

The man's name was Jake. It turned out that he played hockey for the Moose Jaw Canucks. He gave me a couple of tickets to the next game against the Regina Pats. I didn't go to the game but I hoped they won.

# Northland Pro
*Gary Hyland*

My father said the Northland Pro was the world's finest hockey stick. This back when I was shorter than the boards on the outdoor rink and he was still skating for the Hornets. That's when he bought his only Northland. Mother cursed it—a sliver of wood worth more than half a ton of coal.

He showed me how to judge the lie the grain, the splice the shaft for flex and strength, how to space and roll the tape and seal it, sizzling, on the stove. To keep the moisture out, he varnished it, then stood it, perfect and golden, by his equipment in the spare room. At night when he was at work, I'd creep in and hold it, so incredibly light and balanced, smell the mix of varnish, tape and wood and feel the hat tricks flying from its blade. Too beautiful to ice with the cheaper hacking sticks, the gouging of steel.

Each year, even after he'd hung up his skates and I was playing on the high school team, he'd sip beer, add another coat of varnish and talk to that Northland about what they could have done and might yet do. But he got stuck on night shifts and rye and never did see me play, even after he retired, the curved blade and fibreglass days. When he died, the Northland passed to me. It sits in the closet of my den, and once a winter, even now that I've hung up my skates, I open a beer, take it out, dust the darkening wood, and tell it what we might have done.

## The B-P-T

*Gary Hyland*

Two 3's fixed on the scoreboard
Two minutes left, last game of the finals
I pick up a rebound beside our net. spot
Our centre breaking, bank one off the boards
which their winger takes in stride and slaps
hard and high into our net for the winner.

Half an hour later, most of the guys gone,
I'm still in skates when Gord, the coach,
Taps my ankle, mutters, "B-P-T"
And slouches from the dressing room.

I swore not to return for the next season
But I loved the game and managed to con
Myself into believing I'd improved enough
To be considered average and wouldn't puke
Before, after or during games. My decision
Brought out the sadist in Gord. One night
He explains the B-P-T to the whole team.

"Sports doctors found some players panic at key times. Seize right up, make dumbass plays. Turns out they found these guys got a special anatomical quirk—a super long tendon connecting their right ankle bone to this bit of brain they try to think with." The bugger keeps glancing right at me. "Under pressure, this tendon tightens so when they moved their legs their brains disconnect. That's the Brain Pulling Tendon. B- P- T for short." The guys have a snigger.

I knew he was right. Except it was an ocean of adrenalin drowning a speck of confidence that shot me into chaos or paralysis, not some freak tendon. Same difference though.

# The Reluctant Black Hawk
*Brenda Zeman*

So you want to find the Indian guy who walked out on the Chicago Black Hawks 30 years ago? Good luck. Freddie Sasakamoose has no phone. Nor does he return a phone message passed on to him by his friend, Ray Ahenakew. Maybe, you think, he's had his fill of strangers asking him why he gave up a Canadian boy's dream to play in the National Hockey League. Yet, because you want to understand how it happened, you decide to jump in your car, go look for this Freddie Sasakamoose, track him down.

You head north from Saskatoon into Doukhobor country beyond the North Saskatchewan River. In the Lucky Dollar store at Blaine Lake, a fair-haired woman looks at you, then says "Nyet" to a baby fussing in a grocery cart.

North of town, past the Muskeg Lake Reserve sign, you veer northwest. The road is paved and bales of hay and swaths of wheat lie on golden hills set into the blue sky. To your relief, you see people ahead, a road crew. You ask directions but even the road crew doesn't seem to know the road. About 30 miles, says one fellow. Sixty, for sure, says another. A third says, "Better ask at the garage this side of Shell Lake."

Simonar's Repair Service and Cafe. The old garage man eyes you curiously when you say you want to go to Sandy Lake.

"I'm looking for Freddie Sasakamoose," you add.

"So am I," he says.

"Why?"

"He owes me," he drawls, his face crinkling into a slow smile, no sign of malice in his tired blue eyes.

Three teenage girls stand hitchhiking on a reserve road. You stop and they pile in. They don't know much about Freddie Sasakamoose. One girl says he used to be chief of Sandy Lake and he used to play for the Sandy Lake Chiefs.

That's all you know? you ask. What about the slapshot? What about his ambidexterity? The rink-long rushes? His magic on the ice?

The girls are puzzled and they giggle, not knowing what to say. No, they've never heard about Freddie going to Chicago when the NHL only had six teams. Or about the time in 1974 when Freddie was in Edmonton making final preparations to take a young Saskatchewan Indian hockey team to Finland. Howie Meeker heard about it and invited Freddie to a Team Canada (World Hockey Association) practice. Later, in the dressing room, Bobby Hull greeted Freddie with "I know who you are! You're the Indian who played with Chicago. You're the beggar with the slapshot I had to live up to!"

You drive on in the silence wondering what is beyond the next hill. From the top you see the centre of the reserve, a cluster of buildings just down the road. You breathe a sigh of relief.

The name "Ahtahkakoop" is everywhere. On the rink, on the school, finally at the entrance to the band office. After the hereditary chief, one girl says. You ask why the name "Sasakamoose" isn't on the rink, but the girls get out saying they don't know.

You go in the band office and ask for Freddie Sasakamoose, former elected chief of the Ahtahkakoop Indian Reserve. "He's in there," a man points to a door three steps away. At an all-day meeting, he says. "Only happens once a month." He goes inside to get him. You notice a sign in the office: NO LONG DISTANCE TELEPHONE CALLS.

Councillor Freddie Sasakamoose emerges from the meeting room. Your eyes meet at the same level; he can't be more than five feet seven inches tall in his Texaco cap and he's stocky. He doesn't know you from Eve. You tell him you've come to find him, to ask him if he'll tell his story. His black eyes are amused. "Oh yeah," he grins, "I was gonna phone you sometime."

You find yourself grinning with Frederick George Sasakamoose.

## Freddie

I was born December 25, 1933, over at Whitefish Reserve, now they call it Big River Reserve, just neighbourly out from here, about 15 miles from this reserve, Sandy Lake. My mother's father, old Gaspar Morin, lived at Victoire. It used to be a Metis settlement near Whitefish. My grandmother Morin was an Indian from Sandy Lake who married out to a Metis. That made my mother

Metis too, until she married in to a Sandy Lake Indian. My mother's name is Sugil.

Them days in the '30s it was tough. My father, Roderick Sasakamoose, was into loggin'. Very hardly did I see my old man trap. His father was Alexander Sasakamoose and he married a Favel, Julia was my grandmother. Old Alexander musta been into some farming. I remember the time he chased me for jumpin' on some haystacks. He was mute, he couldn't talk or hear, but he could run, that old man. Caught me too, and gave me a good lickin'.

I had a good childhood, real good. It musta been 1937 or '38. I had these bobskates. Old Gaspar used to clean up the ice for me ta skate. It wasn't long till I started makin' hockey sticks from red willows. I'd find a branch, one that was crooked at the end, and chop it off. I'd use any damn thing I could find for a puck. Stones or rocks or cans. Maybe even a frozen apple or two, eh?

Trouble was we didn't have too many horses in them days. Or any good transportation. That was one of the reasons I missed quite a bit of school. I went to school in this area for about a year. What made it tough, I had to walk two and a half miles in the morning and then home again. Five miles in the winter, that was too much for a little guy.

When I was about eight years old, my parents sent me to school at St. Michael's over at Duck Lake. Maybe they seen something ahead for me, I don't know. It wasn't too far away, only about 60 miles, but it seemed like the other end of the world away.

## Sugil

I really missed my kids when I had to send them so far away from home. I had 11 kids but only five lived. I've lost two sets of twins and another boy and another girl, they all died from illness. I knew Freddie and the others would be well taken care of at the residential school. It was better I send them because we didn't have no bus and I didn't want them to get sick. I've sent all my children away to school, including Clara, who was five when she left.

I never went to school and my late husband only a little bit. I never learned to read or write at all until my husband showed me how to play bingo. One night I won $2,800. I spent it in the best way possible, on household things, and I put the rest in the bank.

My mother, her name was Veronica Bear, she raised us really good. My dad, he was Joe Morin, he died when I was about eight. Later my mother married another Morin, this time Gaspar. Anyway, she raised us alone. She taught us not to steal, not to do anything wrong. In fact, she used to always tell me, Sugil, that's my nickname, my real name is Judith, she'd say, Sugil, if you don't do this right, the cops are gonna come and get you!

My mother taught us to do a lot of things, to bake bread, to make bannock, to sew and how to make moccasins. A lot of times when I used to do beadwork, she would rip it out, tell me it wasn't good enough. She would make me do it properly. I guess my mother was right in bringing me up the way she did.

I always tried to do the right thing. But sometimes, even if you try to do the right thing, things go wrong. One day three of us ladies decided to go pickin' berries up north. My friend Alice picked us up in her van. Alice didn't know she had guns in the back, they belonged to her son. After a while we decided we were gonna stay overnight. We didn't know whose place it was but there was bedding and everything we needed right in the cabin.

Next morning we decided to start pickin' berries. But the game warden came. He saw the guns in the van and he charged us a hundred dollars for illegal possession. We decided to pay up on the spot because we didn't want to go to court. We didn't want to be in the newspapers.

The game warden took our hundred dollars and the guns to the RCMP barracks at Big River. It wasn't until Alice's son wondered where his guns had gone to, we had to tell. Pretty soon everyone knew about it. Now they call us 'The Outlaws.'

None of my children were outlaws like me! I tried to pass down all the good qualities from my mother. I think Freddie tried to do his best in hockey. I remember my husband and I used to listen to the radio. My husband was a great sportsman in his day, a really good soccer player for this reserve. He used to travel all around and he scored lots of goals, just like Freddie did in hockey. Anyway, my husband and I used to listen to the radio. I didn't understand many words but I used to hear 'Chicago' and 'Sasakamoose, Sasakamoose,' so

I knew Freddie was good. I don't know why he quit. He never talked about it. My husband and I were kind-hearted, we never spoke in anger to each other, we never asked him about it.

But I know one thing. The reason he played hockey so well is because his Indian name is *Ayahkokopawiwiyin*. My Indian name is Red Thunder Woman. When I hear thunder, I am not afraid, I enjoy it. My youngest son Leo was given the name Morning Star. He is calm and quiet, that makes Leo a good golfer. Freddie got his name from Bertha Starblanket, she's an old woman on this reserve, more than a hundred now. I know Freddie had strong legs for hockey because the old lady named him according to the spirit of a young bull. His Indian name means 'to stand firm.'

## Freddie

Maybe three times I tried to run away from St. Michael's School. Once there were three of us boys. We started out in the morning and we hid out until 3 or 4 o'clock. It was spring and there used to be a ferry just south of Dakota Lake called Carlton Ferry. This ferryman wouldn't cross us. He knew we were from that school. He'd delay us, give us something to eat and he'd grab hold of the phone and call up those priests. Sure enough, in about an hour, the priests would show up and take us back to school. In them days, priests were tough. They shaved our heads and made us sit in the middle of the floor on the cement to embarrass us. All the kids would watch us sittin' there eatin', even the girls.

We were also punished for speaking Cree at school. Whipped sometimes. We did not speak very good English at that time and I still don't. We had a hell of a time tryin' to communicate in English with our fellow little students. We'd usually talk Cree when we were away from the scene, eh? Today I speak Cree real good, it's what I was born with and I enjoy it.

We didn't have no excuse for running away. We were bein' fed good and were bein' treated right. In about seven or eight years after the priests and the sisters had offered me everything into my life, I didn't feel so bad about school. But I wouldn't go back to that kind of system. I guess when you're young like that, you like to come back home. I was lonesome.

Come August I never wanted to go back to school but my parents were determined. They wanted me to be somebody education-wise. And then there was hockey, hockey was the main issue for me. And for the priests too. They were French and a lot of them were from down east, eh, from Montreal, and they were crazy about hockey.

I remember Father Roussel. He believed in a system of obedience. He was just like a Russian trainer. What would happen is that old Father Roussel had maybe 50 pucks in the middle of the bloody ice and if a guy was coastin', not movin' on the whistle, Father Roussel would fire a puck right at him. Of course, when it gets 20 or 30 below, these pucks freeze and in them days we didn't have no padding, everything was homemade, maybe just a few sticks here and there in your pants to stop you from gettin' hit on your charleyhorse.

Father Roussel, he taught me to shoot both ways. I started out shootin' right but one year he was kinda short on left wing. So he says, Who can shoot left? I says, I'll try. Wouldn't you know, it ends up I'm better shootin' left than right.

You know Father Roussel used to say, you gonna hate my guts through the year round. You gonna hate it 'cause I'm gonna train you hard, call the extra effort outta you. But at the end of the season you're gonna thank me. And that's what happened.

## Father Georges Roussel OMI

I first met Frederick Sasakamoose in September 1944, when he was a student at St. Michael's in Duck Lake. I came there to teach and was in charge at the mission at Batoche across the river. I was also sports director and in charge of the brass band too.

I was born in Saskatchewan 12 miles south of St. Walburg. My first language is French, eh? I started teaching in a country school and then I went down to St. Johns College which is now part of the University of Alberta. After that I took a one-year apprenticeship at St. Laurent in Manitoba. From there, I went six years to Lebret and then to Duck Lake.

As you would know, the Oblates were the first ones to help the Indians to receive some education; it was not the government! We have been criticized for taking them out of their cultural milieu. But we had so little money and they were so scattered. At the Indian school in Duck Lake, for example, we had students from Muskeg Lake, Mistawasis, Sandy Lake, Montreal Lake, Sturgeon Lake, Fort a la Corne plus the odd one from some other place.

From the very beginning you noticed Frederick Sasakamoose. He played in the brass band, trombone or bass, something big to make a lot of noise! He was puffing, all right, sometimes his notes were not correct but he seemed to enjoy it.

He showed more promise on the ice. Let's put it this way, let's acknowledge the gifts that God has given to us. I was quite observant. I could quickly see the strong points and the weak points of my players. As well, I know my own strong points and weak points. Frederick was kind of short and stout, he was taller than he was wide, of course, but I would say he was the short strong type.

He had strong legs, he was steady on his skates and had some nice motions feigning to the right or left. I realized that right away. Lots of time when he was a boy, he came to me and said, When I get older I will be playing in the NHL. And in his case I believed it and I would answer, If you work hard, you will succeed. Do your best and play cleanly.

There was only once I had to discipline Frederick and he learned his lesson. He was playing dirty. He got beat by the other guy who managed to bypass him. So he tripped him and that was against my regulations. Our reputation as clean hockey players was good, excellent, I would say. No dirty stuff. Oh, there was some checking, but no bulldozing or ramming into the boards.

Afterwards, the boys were all sitting in the dressing room and I was maybe eight, 10 feet away from Frederick. I said, This isn't the way to play, and I threw a glove in his direction. I could throw straight enough. Of course, it peeved him, naturally. He said, If that's the case, I won't play anymore and you'll lose the game. I answered, I prefer to lose honourably than to win in a shameful way.

The next day was a nice day. Usually, at noon, I'd give the senior team a hockey practice. When it was warm, everybody outside! Take exercise, run around, shoot some snowballs, whatever, but get some oxygen to the brain!

Frederick stayed in on the first day. On the second day, he was standing by the window so he could see us on the rink. The third day he came out and stood along the boards. He was shouting at the boys, Come on, hurry up, get going! Hockey was getting the best of him.

When I came in, Frederick was standing firmly in the doorway, blocking my entrance. He said, If you want me to, I'll play. I said, If you want to do what I tell you, okay. If not, no deal. He said, I will, and from that time, no trouble.

He followed my orders from that time on. I believe in conditioning. I used to give the boys gymnastics, bench work and some mat work. They did a lot of running when the ice was bad, and I had them roller-skating in the off-season. When the ice was good, I'd get them out skating. I could skate enough to move ahead. To make them move, I'd use my hockey stick, a little tap to the seat, not a big one, for ones who were lagging behind. The boys used to enjoy that. They'd say, Look at him, slowpoke, go after him. Shoot the puck at them? No, well, maybe shoot towards them, on the side. I could shoot straight enough.

As for Frederick's shot, I believe in the wrist shot, quick and accurate. Frederick developed a good, excellent, I would say, wrist shot when he played at St. Michael's. He practised all the time, even taking practice with the younger boys when I was too busy. I would say Frederick lived for hockey. And so did the other boys on the team.

You know, those who say the Russians showed us how to play hockey don't know what they are talking about. In 1948, Joe Primeau, he was a scout for the Toronto Maple Leafs, he saw my boys play in a provincial championship game in Weyburn. My boys were like scrubs, so short compared to the Weyburn boys. But we had all but two returning the next year. Joe Primeau said to me, Father, your boys do not play as fast as the professionals but they play positional hockey.

And that was true. Frederick knew what he was doing on the ice by the time he left St. Michael's. He had confidence. The exciting thing about watching Frederick was this: you knew he was going to score. You just didn't know his plan of attack. And that provided the suspense. Maybe, when he got to Chicago, he didn't work hard enough or maybe he married too young. I don't think Frederick would mind me saying this, I've been to his house and he received me well several times, but maybe his heart took him out of the play.

## Freddie

In the spring of 1949, we beat Regina and won the midget championship of Saskatchewan, eh? That's when I thanked Father Roussel. That time was something I'll never forget. Of course, the team rode back to the school in one of those big damn grain trucks we used to use, squeezin' together to keep warm.

After that I came back home and I had no intention of goin' into junior hockey. None at all. Never had no dream. You just go back home, that's all. Maybe we figured we weren't good enough to go to junior hockey training camp. Our dream was never NHL, never.

I was back here in the fall, about this time of year. We were stookin' over at Blue Heron, my mom and dad and me, it was threshin' time. All of a sudden a car pulled into the field and I thought I seen Father Roussel comin'. I thought he was comin' to take me back to school and I said to my dad, Oh, no, I'm not goin' back. I'm 15 and I'll be 16 in December and I don't have to go back.

Ends up it was Father Chevrier, he was gonna be boss at Duck Lake, and two other guys. He said, D'ya wanna go to trainin' camp in Moose Jaw? And I said, Where's that?

When he told me where, I said, No, I'm not goin'. No damn way was I gonna go any place now that I'm back home. Then Father Chevrier says, I'll tell you what, I'll give you $50 a month for spendin' money and I'll dress you up real good. I still wasn't going to go. I thought he was talkin' about those old combination overalls the sisters used to make us at Duck Lake.

Finally, Mom came over and Dad came over. He says, You have a good offer. After about an hour of coaxin', my mother demanded that I go and I gave up. I musta done good in Moose Jaw, I showed up real good, I musta. That's when George Vogan of the Canucks told me to come live with him and his wife Flora and his daughter Phyllis. Treated me real good, those people.

## Phyllis Vogan Hendry

My dad was the general manager of the Moose Jaw Canucks. I was 16 at the time. I came home late one night and I heard something in the living room. I went upstairs and asked my brother's girlfriend—she was visiting from Michigan where my brother was playing minor pro—I asked her who was in the living room. Phyllis, she said, your father brought home another hockey player and this time he's an Indian!

Just a few days before, the same girl and I had gone to the train station because my father was out of town and he asked us to go meet Ray Leacock, a defenceman from Montreal. Ray was surprised I spotted him so quickly on the platform. Ray, I said, you're probably the only black guy in Moose Jaw. For sure you're the only one in a hockey jacket. This was too much for my brother's girlfriend, first Ray, then an Indian fellow. She was American, eh?

You better get used to it, I told her, that's the way we do things in this house.

I got up the next morning and there was Freddie. He had on a pair of real heavy plaid pants and a thick plaid shirt and a cap pulled down over his ears, Anyway, there he sat, looking just terrified. About like Metro Prystai looked when he'd come to live with us about seven years before.

Freddie had never seen plumbing so that night I told Dad, You better take him up and show him how to use the bathtub. We'd done that with Metro. So Dad took him up. Freddie's mom had made him black silk shorts and that's how Dad left him in the bathroom. Freddie was in there for about an hour and a half. Finally I said, Dad, you better go see what he's doing in there. Dad went and there was Freddie sitting in an empty tub in his black silk shorts.

But Freddie learned very quickly, he was very bright. He was such a beautiful handwriter. He used to write "Frederick Sasakamoose" over everything, sheets, tablecloths, you name it, until one day I said, Freddie, I don't care if you're practising your autograph, this has got to stop. The other thing I was really impressed with was Freddie's reflexes. He used to catch our budgie out of the air as it flew past him. And he could throw five pennies in the air and catch them before they hit the floor.

Freddie wasn't the first Indian person to live with us. One day in about 1943, Dad showed up at the house with an American Indian. Dad ran into

Chief Iktomi in Fir Mountain. The chief had about six university degrees and he was going around doing a book on North American Indians until his tires were flat at Fir Mountain. Tires were hard to come by during the war so Dad offered to help get him some tires. Ended up the chief moved in with us and Metro and the other eight hockey players and stayed with us for six months.

Freddie lived with us for four years, three years with Mom and Dad, and when my husband and I got married, he moved in with us next door for a year. Freddie couldn't have lived with just anybody in those days. He needed to be looked after in lots of ways. He was so honest he'd always pay up what he owed at Doraty's pool hall. Once he came home and said, Phyl, I lost a hundred dollars and I paid up but there's two guys owe me more than that and they won't pay up. They were orderlies from the hospital and I had to call up the Mother Superior. She forced them to pay up.

Money literally flew by Freddie. I remember after he went up to Chicago for a few games in the spring of '53. He came home with a big cheque and he wasn't supposed to cash it till he got to Saskatchewan. When he got here, almost the first thing he shows me is a big photo of a beautiful Indian model. I think he said she was Cherokee, he'd met her in Chicago. She was modelling something pretty scanty in the photo and I thought, Oh boy, Freddie, you may be in the big leagues but this girl is outta your league!

When Freddie lived with us, hockey was his life. He socialized with the rest of the team, but always as a part of the group, you know, everybody going out and having a good time together. I remember he used to correspond with an Indian girl named Rose, a nursing student, I think, and an Isbister girl named Loretta from up north. But he rarely saw them and it was more a friendship thing. Still, this girl from Chicago was supposed to have him running around missing practices.

Anyway, next day after Freddie got to Moose Jaw, he went out and bought a big car with the cash he had on him. He still had his cheque when he headed off to Humboldt to see Rose.

He didn't make it. I got a frantic call, well, about as frantic as Freddie ever got. Phyl, he said, my tire went flat and when I was changing the tire the wind came along and blew my cheque away. What am I gonna do, Phyl? he says.

Dad phoned Chicago right away to put a stop payment on the cheque and I phoned "The Mailbag" on CHAB Moose Jaw to tell people to be on the lookout for a Chicago Black Hawk cheque made out to Freddie Sasakamoose. Wouldn't you know it? A farmer found it in his field and called up the radio station.

I called Freddie and he said, But Phyl, I gotta go see Rose. I said, Freddie, you go get that cheque and thank the man for his trouble. He went, but that was Freddie. He lived for the moment.

Haven't seen Freddie since he was on his way to see Rose. But I remember getting a Christmas card and him telling me he'd named his oldest daughter, Phyllis, after me and his oldest son, Elgin, after a friend of his in Moose Jaw. Freddie was happy here, he was part of our family. When he left for Chicago, I said to Tiny Thompson, the scout, I said, Tiny, they won't care about Freddie in Chicago the way we care about him here.

## Freddie

The year I went to Chicago, we'd lost out in junior hockey to Regina or somebody. I was in the Canuck dressing room takin' my stuff off. Nobody was talkin'. We were sad about bein' taken out. I was thinkin' about goin' home.

First person I seen was George Vogan. That man and his family offered me everythin'. He was just like my dad, and my dad was a good man. George walked towards me, he had a suitcase. I said, What's this, George? He said, Didn't you hear the good news? I said, Nobody ever told me anything yet. Well, he didn't tell me, he just kinda looked around a little bit at the coach and the manager.

All of a sudden the manager came up to me and said, Here's a telex. Here's your plane ticket. You're goin' to Chicago Black Hawks the remainder of the season.

So I didn't know what to do. I just stood there and I looked at the players. They were astonished, me bein' an Indian to be called and go play in the big leagues. Then people walked in there with a watch and my name engraved and a ring with two suitcases filled with clothes so I'd look respectable on my way in. It was a real joy.

## Metro Prystai

I was the first guy to go from the Vogans to the NHL. I was a lot like Freddie, Moose Jaw flabbergasted me, such a big place. And radios and indoor toilets. I thought I was in heaven. In Yorkton we had a crystal set and when nature called we just ran a hundred feet from the house to the biffy. My mother and father didn't speak much English, so my mother said in Ukrainian, My Metro can go to Moose Jaw if he goes to school, he goes to church and he doesn't get paid much to play hockey. She didn't need to worry about me bein' a good boy. Instead of going to the pool hall, I'd go skating every night. It was indoors and it was free.

I was gone from Moose Jaw by the time Freddie moved in with the Vogans. I was 19 when I went up to Chicago in 1947. A couple of years later George Vogan started telling me about this great kid Sasakamoose, what a helluva hockey player he was and I started seeing him in the spring when I'd drive from Chicago to Saskatchewan with Doug Bentley.

## Freddie

I took the plane the next day. I'd never been on a plane before. I met the team in Toronto. Some of the people from Moose Jaw followed me too. They wanted to see me play. I got in the dressing room and they gave me number 16 and I didn't know what the heck to do.

Anyway, I got on the ice and I was skatin' around warmin' up. At the time I was just like a ... I'm not braggin', but I could skate and skate and shoot, real good. I had my slapshot by then. I don't know where it come from. I don't know where I seen it. Nobody was usin' it much then. It just came natural to me. So I took a shot or two and a referee come up to me and says, Somebody wants to talk to you on the phone. I went over to the penalty box and some guy said over the phone, How the hell do you pronounce your damn name? Saskatchewan Moose? Sack-a-Moose? Sask-a-moose? I said, Who am I talkin' to? And the voice said, Foster Hewitt. My gosh, I said, Foster! You know, I heard so much about Foster. Back home and at the school we used to listen to Saturday night hockey all the time. So I was talkin' to Foster and I gave him my name properly, Sa-sa-ka-moose, and I guess that's how he done it, bein' professional he was. I was in the big time now.

## Metro Prystai

I'd been traded to Detroit by the time Freddie went up to Chicago. Chicago wasn't doin' that well at the time and Freddie was supposed to be the saviour. Since he'd done so well in amateur hockey, he was supposed to pick up the franchise. And, of course, management made a big ballyhoo about him bein' the first treaty Indian to make the NHL. They wanted Freddie to fill Chicago Stadium.

I know Freddie musta been afraid when he first went up. I know I was. He had to contend with jumpin' right from junior to the NHL and he had to contend with Chicago. And that was scary. Ya gotta remember, Al Capone died in prison from syphilis the year before I went up to Chicago. And then Freddie had to contend with livin' at the Midwest Athletic Club. We all did. I had to live there too when I played with Chicago.

They called it a hotel but really it was a dive. They had a place downstairs where gamblers used to hang out. It was a boxing club. I remember one guy fought under the name of Rudy Valentino. And all these hoodlums used to sit at ringside in their white and black fedoras. The gangsters used to feel sorry for us poor hockey players. They used to tell us they could get us jobs payin' a lot more. But I wasn't gonna carry a gat like those guys...

The biggest gangster I ever ran into at the Midwest was Matty Capone, Al's younger brother. Once, when I was playing for Detroit, Matty was in the crowd. I tried to avoid skating by his corner of the rink but he kept calling me over. I was afraid to go and I was afraid not to. Finally, I went and he says real tough-like, Hey, Metro, get me an autographed stick. I got him an autographed stick.

I remember Detroit playin' a home-and-home series with Chicago shortly after Freddie cracked the lineup. There'd been a lot of publicity and when Freddie came out, there was a big cheer. I was glad I wasn't playing defence or goal against him. He had a very hard, very accurate slapshot and his wrist shot, well, he could get away with nothin'. A lot of guys have to wind up, but not

Freddie. He had tremendous wrists. He could be fallin' down and still get a good shot away. And he could skate. He could stop and start on a dime and he could hit top speed in two, maybe three strides. He had the best reflexes I've ever seen, better'n Gordie Howe.

It's hard to know why I lasted and he didn't. But I know one thing. If he'd been with a better organization, maybe like Toronto or Montreal or Detroit, they could have afforded to bring him along more slowly, they could've groomed him better. Chicago's general manager, Bill Tobin, wasn't the hockey man that Conn Smythe, Frank Selke or Jack Adams were. Freddie was most likely with the wrong organization.

I remember, though, when I was with Chicago we used to joke in the dressing room about Doug Bentley, he sorta had a big nose, eh? Nothing against it at all, but we used to tease him about being the only Black Hawk with a picture of himself on the front of his sweater. Then, we'd say, When Freddie Sasakamoose comes up, he'll be the real thing. Doug used to laugh, he kinda enjoyed it.

## Freddie

I don't know how in hell I ever come to have a crest like that one, me bein' a treaty Indian and playin' for Chicago Black Hawks.

Chicago was really somethin'. It kinda helped me along with city life, havin' lived in Moose Jaw. In Chicago you were just like another joe walkin' down the street. In Moose Jaw you knew who you were. Freddie Sasakamoose. But in Chicago nobody knew you.

I guess some of the hockey people knew me. When I played my first game in Chicago I ended up on TV and they gave me a transistor radio and a box of cigars. That night about 19,000 people come and see the Indian play. And when I first walked in, the organist started playin' the Indian Love Call. He was kinda a comical fella.

In Chicago I stayed in a hotel and I used to have a friend who roomed with me called Jerry Toppazzini. He used to take me all over. Once he took me to shake hands with Louis Armstrong. Another time I remember standin' in the doorway talkin' with Jack Dempsey in his restaurant in New York. I just don't know about it, I met some of the great ones.

When I come back after playin' for those first two months I had a little bit of money, about seven, eight thousand dollars. When I turned pro they gave me three thousand and I had to sign the "C" form to be affiliated with Chicago. Maybe it was ten thousand, I don't know, it was so damn long ago. Then they gave me the day wages of that time, about a hundred and fifty a day plus room and board.

I come back home that spring after I turned pro. I bought a car. I never owned no car, I used to take cabs. I bought a big DeSoto, a fluid drive, and everyone knew I was back. You shoulda seen me when I walked into this reserve when I come from Chicago when I was 19. It was just like I was outta this world. People looked at you, amazed. It was a wonderful feeling. It's something I have to thank the Creator for, my younger life. Jesus, I was called from all over to play exhibition games, a hundred dollars a game. There was still ice in Saskatchewan and every place I went was filled. I was young and I was single and everyone wanted to see me play.

## Loretta Sasakamoose

I thought it was pretty good of Freddie to come and see me, little Loretta Isbister from Bodmin, when he could have had almost anybody, eh? We kinda got together through my brothers. They had this thing about Freddie. Whenever he played hockey, they wanted to go see him because he was such a good player. We lived out in the sticks and my dad farmed, mixed farming. My mother was from Sandy Lake Reserve till she married my dad, Miles Isbister, he's Metis. Then automatically, she was classified as non-Indian. In her heart she was always Indian and to us, we classified ourselves as Indian too because there's not much difference with Metis and Indian.

My mother died when I was 14, which was tragic for all of us. From then on I raised my youngest six brothers and sisters. There was no one else to do it. I was young but you grow up pretty fast when you have to.

I was 16 when I met Freddie and he was 18. I think there was quite a bit of difference there. I was kinda tied up at home whereas he was from one city to another seeing all those places. But we hit it off real good as friends and he'd write letters to me and send me a Christmas present, a Valentine's card, this and that.

My brothers were really happy when I married Freddie four years later. But I don't know about my dad. Well, you know, most dads have this thing of trying to hang on to their girl for as long as they can. I have raised the family and probably they hated to see me go. Leaving them behind I sorta felt like I was neglecting them and, finally, my dad said, You did your share for this long and it's fine. But I still had that feeling.

The thought of going to Chicago was a bit much. I don't know much about cities and at that time I didn't know nothing about big cities! There's a lot of good things about people here. They tend to be a little backward, a little shy. You can't just say, I'll make a friend here, I'll make a friend there. It just wasn't in me.

You know, I even had a hard time moving from the south end of Sandy Lake to the north end when we built this new log house. The old house, that was where we raised our nine children, where Freddie started farming, and we had the three buses. He started getting machinery little by little and now don't ask me how many acres he's farming! After we moved here, I'd find myself back at the old house two or three times a day and it's only seven or eight miles away! I even spent a couple nights there last year and I had a very good sleep. But now, we've been here better than a year and I like it now. This is the place we'll raise our second family as long as our son-in-law wants us to. Our oldest daughter passed away three years ago. Oh, it was so hard on all of us, especially on Freddie. Now we have her three children to remember her by.

The only time I've ever been away was when I lived for three years with Freddie in Kamloops. I read and I read and I read when I was alone during the day. At night there were times we'd sit together and Freddie would say, It's so lonely, Loretta, I'll be glad when hockey season's over.

## Freddie

I was in the '55 Chicago training camp in Welland and I was expectin' some letters from Loretta, we'd just been married July 22 that summer. Every day I looked and there was nothin'. I kept on wondering about my old lady and what was gonna become of her. I'd phone her, of course we had no telephone, so I'd have to phone the store. Somehow or other I couldn't get her on the phone. After about 20 days I got worried. What the hell am I gonna do? And I was just doin' so good in training camp.

About 10 days before 30-day camp was over, I got a hold of my wife. I said, I'm gonna make the team, Loretta, now you come over here. I got a house all ready, I'm makin' good money. She held back, she didn't want to come. She told me no. Well, then it was a problem. I had to talk to the management, Tommy Ivan. I said, Tommy, I'm havin' a heck of a time with my old lady, she doesn't want to come to Chicago. Is there by any chance you could send me to Western Canada? Someplace I could be close to my wife, someplace she'd enjoy.

That's when I went to New Westminster to play for the Royals. Kenny MacKenzie was the manager. I said, Kenny, I gotta go for my wife. I want a couple of plane tickets, give me a coupla days and I'll be back in three or four. Away I went.

Got over to Saskatoon airport, phoned a taxi nearby here in Debden and said, Rainey, come and pick me up. So he come and a coupla, three hours later we got back here, about 6, 7 in the morning, it was a little daylight. Got to Loretta's dad's house, everybody sleepin' and I was yellin' from the outside. Knocked on the door, nobody answered, so I went upstairs. Loretta opened the door a little, she knew it was me, ha ha, she said, What do you want? I said, Open the door, I want to talk to you.

She didn't tell anybody about that, ha ha. Maybe I guess she never will but I'm glad I could be able to tell a little bit about it. Anyway, old Miles, my father-in-law, was happy to see me, the old fella. Sat down and had a little breakfast and coffee. Meanwhile, Rainey's waitin' for me in the taxi outside.

After a little while I said, Loretta, I got a couple of tickets here. Want to take you back, got a good house, makin' a good living, about another year or so we'll go back to Chicago and continue playing NHL. And she said no. I don't know what she thought at that time. Still don't.

So I went back to see Mom and Dad and I told them the problems and they said, Well, it's best that you go back. You got a good life, a good future ahead of you, you're young, you done what you wanted to do for the best of her. She didn't want to come so I went back.

I moved to New Westminster, to Calgary, to Chicoutimi—Quebec League—bouncing all over the damn place. I guess maybe it was a little bit of control, that was the problem, not using alcohol, not using anything, just that I kinda fell apart because she wouldn't come with me. My wife was a beautiful girl and I loved her very much.

Two years after, I went back to Calgary and I was playing in Saskatoon in that old western pro league and my mom and dad were there and a few people from the reserve and some Indians in Saskatoon come to watch me play. My mother brought me a beaded jacket, a real beautiful jacket she made for me. My parents were real proud of me, eh, real proud.

Durin' the hockey game I was kinda lookin' around where all the Indians were sittin', tryin' to see my wife. Didn't see her no place. After the game I asked my mom where Loretta was. My mom didn't know why she didn't come.

After, I went back to the hotel. Decided I was gonna go. I was gonna quit right then, pack my gear and go home. I was still affiliated with the Black Hawks. Anything they say I had to do. So I knew this was the end of my playin' NHL, the end of my younger life.

I played this bush league in Debden for a couple years and I lived with Loretta. Then I got a call from Kenny MacKenzie in Kamloops, double-A senior. I got to know the people at the Kamloops Indian Reserve, Loretta was with me and I could still play a little bit of good hockey.

## Muriel Gottfriedson Sasakamoose

I first met Freddie in 1957 when he came to Kamloops to play for the Kamloops Chiefs. Before the hockey season was over, I married his brother Peter.

My reserve, Kamloops Reserve, is situated right across the river from the city of Kamloops. "Kamloops" comes from the Interior Salish world meaning 'meeting of the rivers' and we had a population of about 300 at that time.

People were very impressed by Freddie when he came out there. At first we saw him as a star. We had some real different ideas about him. We didn't think of him as quite human. People were a little bit distant and hesitant to come up to him and be friendly and talk to him. They held him in awe. To Indian people he was the equivalent of Elvis Presley as a celebrity. He was an idol, yet he was a role model for young people. Indian people from all around bought season tickets and filled up a whole section of the Kamloops arena.

To this day he's still the only person from the plains who's ever been made honorary chief of Kamloops Indian Reserve. My band hosted a traditional ceremony. They had dancers come from the Shuswap Nations next to our reserve and from the Thompsons, the Okanagans and the fringes of the Chilcotin tribes. They went on top of Mount Paul and sent signals to all of the tribal groups and they gathered and honoured him. My people named him Chief Thunderstick because Freddie was very famous for his slapshot.

## Freddie

I'd say I was famous, in Indian eyes I was famous. It was a great disappointment that I had given them, I imagine I did. Even the white people in Canwood and Debden were disappointed I was not playing in the NHL, even them, they knew me. But it was more so for my parents because they saw great things in life for me.

The people on this reserve, they treated me real good when I came back. I knew their life, how their world was and how they made their livin'. Of course, I had to learn how to live on the outside. But I didn't want to force that way of life on Indian people. I think you have to leave the Indian people, how they enjoy life, how they enjoy themselves, leave that alone. I adjust myself real good. Not once did I leave this reserve since I come back. Although there's brighter future on the outside, there's freedom here.

You see, when you were playin' hockey, you were never free. You were more or less looked at, told what to do. That's part of life as a professional and you're paid well for it. When I turned pro, I knew damn well I was dressed good, I'd be able to get the things I want. Every two weeks I was gettin' paid and I was gettin' wiser. I was 21, 22 at the time and I thought, Goddamn, I'm gonna make it and I'm gonna go through the life of bein' in the NHL. God, it was good. A lot of times I sat down and asked myself what went wrong with my hockey life. I do not blame it to my wife, I do not blame nobody. Maybe there were just some things I could not adjust to. The only thing, it makes a guy kinda wonder what he coulda done with some of these big contracts today.

## Muriel Sasakamoose

After Peter and I lived for a time at Sandy Lake, I got to know Freddie as a person. He has a lot of self-confidence. He's a survivor. He's also a bit of a trend-setter, you should see his new log house. He's outgoing, he's musical, he plays guitar and sings and he can really dance. Freddie's a good person to have at a party. People crowd around him because he's energetic and he's a good storyteller. Freddie can talk to down-and-outers, drunks, and he can also talk to the Prime Minister of Canada.

Now that I'm a band administrator for Sandy Lake, I get the opportunity to see Freddie in a different light. I'm the first woman to ever hold this office and most people here really felt, you know, me coming from a matrilineal society such as the Interior Salish and this being a very male-oriented society at Sandy Lake, well, they had a hard time adjusting to me. I always thought in terms of women, children and men, the total community, whereas the men tended to think more of what the men wanted to do. The women here are quite silent compared to me. The men often said, That Muriel, she's a woman libber, and a lot of flak came from my brother-in-law Freddie!

Freddie and I realized our differences right away. Freddie tends to be a bleeding heart and he believes every sob story that comes his way. Freddie's a dreamer. I am most often a realist and I sort of say, Give them a swift kick in the ass and that's the direction they should go. But Freddie and I both believe in the community and the betterment of Indian people and see that change has to take place.

I admire Freddie very much. You've got to remember when he first got into hockey, Sandy Lake didn't have roads, telephones or electricity, and there were only two vehicles on this reserve. The only things he really knew were trapping, hunting, farming and hockey. To go from here to Chicago, that's a big jump. And he did it. I really think if he wasn't so tied to his family and his community, he would probably have stayed longer. But it doesn't matter. Freddie gave us all something to be very proud of. But he rarely talks about it. Freddie doesn't live in the past.

## Freddie

If I was to die today, I wouldn't cry for my life. I've met a lot of good people, a lot of good Indians and a lot of good white people. The enemies I created through my hockey life, the fans that called me names, you know, every one of them came back. I know every one of them. I hear them when I'm on the ice, you know. You're an Indian and this and that, but, you know, I never looked. It never hurted me because I always had pride in me. Enemies from that time come up now and shake hands with me and say, remember when I used to call you names? I don't know, I say, did you? Well, I say, that's gone.

Now I meet people who say, Any of your children as good as you were? I don't think so, I say. People look at me and think I should be able to produce all good hockey players. But I never did go out there with my kids and support them by trainin' them.

I lost my oldest daughter three years ago when I was chief. I knew that my daughter was killed in a car accident due to alcohol. At that time I too was drinkin', but not heavy; I was chief. I knew it hurt my life and it hurt my family so I very, very seldom used alcohol.

I was blessed with a good wife. She never drank, she's a beautiful woman, she took care of my children when I was not always there. I'm blessed. Funny thing, I didn't know till I was almost 50. When I lost my daughter, it changed me.

Now I'm 52, almost 53. I'm a community man. I was chief for four years, served my people well. I believe in the system of competition with the outside white society. When I was a kid I learned to compete with the outside and I had to be able to do things twice as good to continue to play hockey with them.

But the thing I remember is comin' home from school every summer, eh? It was wonderful when we come on top of that hill over there. We used to drive up in that big three-ton grain truck, you know, 50 or 60 of us piled in there. About six or seven miles south of here, I could see the hill and at the top, oh boy, what a feeling to see this reserve.

## Old-Timers Hockey
### *Glen Sorestad*

1.
Their thinning hair has gone the colour
of the ice they skate upon. Many are jowly,
double-chinned, solid as Zambonis

They hunch over faceoffs, chinstraps
straining to check the flesh they've
accumulated like minor penalties.

Once as much part of them as their skates,
the quick agility gone with maskless goalies
or one-piece sticks with uncurved blades.

All replaced now by old aches and scars,
battered knees, sore joints, lost resilience—
hard knocks dealt out in life's tight corners.

2.
See their strides—shorter now, more
deliberate, they cajole leaden legs
to move, limbs that long for soft sofas.

They lunge for pucks; passes once fixed
as tape to their sticks now bounce away.
Most of them pass more and stickhandle

Less, having learned—some of them
more slowly, if at all—the pass is
the quickest way to move the puck.

No scores or statistics kept here.
The warriors of hockey-past gather here
three mornings a week to share

Satisfying rituals, the metamorphosis
from worn and drab old men's clothes
into the timelessness of hockey gear.

3.
A few are players of famous teams past,
recognizable to hockey buffs, but most
are unknown—to the others, if not themselves.

A few ex-pros, who dragged their aches
and bruises, swollen and scarred knuckles,
their faces road maps of hockey miles,

sweaty team buses, cheers and catcalls
still reverberating from long-ago arenas
scattered through leagues lost to history.

Here, too, among hockey veterans are
those who never made a team in any league,
who haven't played since boyhood.

Retired from working lives, they mingle
and skate alongside others whose lives
were one long and glorious game.

Each new old-timer released from drudge
must now relearn the rules, the team play,
the give-and-go that makes hockey.

Now in their sixties and seventies, they all
pay the same for using the rink, even those
who once were paid to play the game.

4.
None but their fellows here bear witness
to any small triumph (the perfect pass)
or embarrassment (missing the empty net).

No adoring fans, no watchful scouts,
no trophies at stake to goad their bodies.
They compete—inside each, a game image.

They fear no injury, unless they tumble—
the game is slowed and safe, contact
no longer part of their game. They can

Look down at the puck, exult in a perfect pass,
safe, knowing no vicious check will exact
the penalty for failing to keep the head up.

Sometimes a player takes exception: an errant
stick across the leg, or one comes up too high,
and angry words erupt to mar the goodwill

that marks their game; but bitter feelings
can never linger in a game played only
for what the game affords—camaraderie.

5.
This is a game of slow grace, pattern, beauty.
Little remains of ego and bravado that fired
their youth, little left to hinder the flow

from one to another to another, a movement
determined to take in every player as if passing
the disc back and forth, up and down the ice

were more important than to score. Perhaps it is.
Occasional bursts of speed still set one player
apart a moment, sudden dekes that surprise

as manoeuvres from the past reassert themselves
in this long slowing of blood and bone.
Some puck hogs show up here, too,

but all learn that none here wants to be
a loner; they learn what eluded them years ago:
when you give, you will receive.

6.
Watch awhile: a quiet exuberance.
Boys, eternal youth of frozen sloughs,
outdoor shinny rinks; enduring scorers

from snowy streets under hooded lamps
of a thousand towns; ageless lads,
lugging taped sticks, instead of canes,

hoisting hockey bags, not snow shovels.
Inside each sweater thumps a heart never far
from the puck, nor does it ever want to be.

True boys of hockey, they rag the puck,
stickhandling time off the relentless clock.
They skate, pass, shoot—play for overtime.

## The Northfield Comets
*Allan Safarik*

Things had seemed better than ever back in August when Orville and Del were putting together plans for the coming hockey season. They were shooting their weekly 8-ball match over at the Northfield Hotel. It was a tradition that had endured for over 30 years of Saturday afternoons.

"Should be a pretty fair team!" Orville thundered as he moved his belly around his cue.

Del, officially Delmar Fuchs, had been manager of the Comets since Moses was in prep school.

"Well, Mayor," he intoned, allowing a little shine to rub off on Orville. "With Wolf Slawson coming back to coach, we'll be fast and mean."

Orville left the 8-ball slightly off the rail near the far right-hand end pocket. Del stepped up, tapped his cue toward the pocket. He kissed the edge of the black ball with the white cue ball. The 8-ball trickled down.

"How much do I owe you now?"

"Lemme see," Del said as he squinted into a pocket notebook. "Countin' these three games, Orville, you owe me a little under $382,000."

The news only got better. Raccoon Coogle was over his broken leg. Billy Smiles, who was good for a goal a game, had just been released from jail. Thad MacDonald, nicknamed Onion Head for obvious reasons, had decided to put off retiring for another year.

"What the hell, 44 ain't too old. What would I do all winter?"

Onion Head, a slow stay-at-home defenceman, guarded the slot in front of his own net with the instincts of a wolverine. T-Bar Kelly, the flashy boy goalie, was still working at the Petro-Can. People were encouraged seeing him out behind the garage stopping shots. Best of all, Dwayne Semple had left the army and decided to return home to help farm with his dad. Semple, a wiry offensive-minded defenceman, would lead the league in scraps and assists. He would be "captain" because he would log the most ice time. Del was loving it.

He could see the Wheatland Hockey League trophy glistening in its place of honour at the Northfield rink. Everyone figured having Wolf Slawson behind the bench was worth at least a one-goal advantage. No referee in his right mind ever trifled with Wolf. All his great moments in life had occurred in the midst of mayhem on a sheet of ice. Fans on the road taunted him from across the rink. When Wolf's large lupine personality confronted them at close range, they either meekly called him sir or wet their pants.

When Orville and Del drove over to Bluffsville for the annual Wheatland Hockey League meeting, they knew trouble was brewing. League commissioner Aubrey Shanks was a horrible homer who twisted league bylaws into his own personal agenda of justice. Shanks hosted the meeting in his barbershop. He waited until all the governors were in place on the rickety wooden chairs beside the pile of Reader's Digests. Shanks had the hands of a beautician and a voice that could melt rust from car fenders.

"Now boys, we'll have to have a small fee increase to cover the commissioner's office."

They all listened politely and thought why not? Shanks' daughter Eloise took care of scheduling for eight teams and she kept league statistics. Mrs. Shanks took all the team pictures, handled league PR and kept Shanks sober during the playoffs.

"One more thing," Shanks' voice took on a harsher tone and raised up in volume. "I'm not happy about Wolf Slawson coaching in this league. The man's demented. I told you boys from the Comets to get rid of him last year."

Orville and Del exchanged glances. They had been trying to sink Shanks for 10 years.

Del stood up. "Wolf's our coach, Aubrey. He behaved real good last year. Why, there was only that one little incident when he bit that woman in Fairweather."

Orville chimed in with, "Yeah, while she was fixin' to clobber him with a length of pipe."

Shanks moved behind the barber chair. "Just so you know my feelings on Wolf. I'll suspend him fast if he even burps at a referee. By the way, since you're all here, anybody need a haircut?"

Before the season started, Orville and Del took Wolf aside and told him to cool it. They figured the Comets would eat up the league, might as well save the rough stuff for the playoffs. Del thought of a slogan that Wolf could use to motivate the players. He got Polly to make a sign for the dressing room wall. It read, COMETS PLAY IT TOUGH, FAST, AND CLEAN. Orville and Del carried the sign over to the rink. The players were just coming off the ice after the first practice of the season. Billy Smiles was honking in the garbage can. Onion Head was unimpressed. "About as inspiring as the foaming cleanser," he remarked. Wolf left talking to himself.

By the end of the first month of the season, the Comets were mired in a five-game losing streak. In the first three games, T-Bar played his heart out. The rest of the team was sluggish and unable to perform. Billy Smiles had lost his scoring touch. Raccoon Coogle's leg was killing him. In Game 4, T-Bar with his butterfly style went into the toilet bowl, allowing four goals in less than three minutes of the second period. To make matters worse, Dwayne, who was fifth in league scoring, had had his nose broken twice. Onion Head looked like he was skating in a cat box. In Game 5, T-Bar was displaying lucky pink rabbit's feet attached to each of his leg pads. Wolf was pacing around in Del's storeroom like a wild animal in awful pain. Del was persuading him to try Slim in goal.

"It'll give the boys a different look, besides T-Bar's thinking too much and it might do him good to ride the pine."

"Okay, okay," Wolf agreed. "But if it don't work, we do it my way."

Slim was a gamer but the sound of his knees knocking together through his ancient deer hair pads hardly inspired his teammates. The Black Blades from Bluffsville came into town and registered an 11-3 whipping to the Comets. They made it worse by gooning it up. Del and Orville said nothing when they encountered Aubrey Shanks smoking a victory cigar in the rink lobby. Aubrey called it "a good old-fashioned tuning."

Orville and Del were sitting in a corner booth at George's Cafe drinking coffee. George brought them the luncheon special.

"Here you go, boys, two chop suey burgers. Anybody care for the catsup?"

Wolf Slawson came in stamping his feet from the cold and muttering 0-and-6 through clenched teeth. When George served him his coffee, Wolf was so distressed he tore the handle right off the cup. Del motioned for calm with his hand.

"Wolf, you're the coach, you call the shots from now on."

"Good, I've got a new slogan to put up in the dressing room."

"What is it?" Orville asked as he devoured half of his hamburger.

Wolf's eyes glazed over and he answered, "IF IT'S MOVING, IT AIN'T DEAD."

George came out from the kitchen and sat at the booth. "I like it," he said. "It's catchy."

Wolf was a pack animal. He understood the old-time pride of small-town hockey players. The first thing he did was grab T-Bar by the throat and take away all his lucky charms, including his voodoo doll and the Playboy centrefold he tucked into his pads.

"No excuses," he said, exhaling his bad breath between T-Bar's eyes. Wolf kicked over the coffee urn. He grabbed Billy Smiles' lit cigarette and butted it into the palm of his own hand. Turning on Raccoon Coogle, he sneered, "Coogle, that leg brace you're wearing would do more good if you wore it on your head." One by one he went around the room. When he got to Onion Head, he snorted, "You may as well head for the rest home the way you're playing." Wolf paused for a few frozen moments to let his tirade sink in. "We're gonna keep it simple. From now on it's dump, chase and staple. Anybody dare put the puck in our net ends up on the slab. Any questions?" There were none, everybody knew their duty. They had seen the weird light in Wolf's eyes before on the bitter winter night he went down after beating up the cops in Rosetown.

Naturally the Comets were more afraid of Wolf Slawson than they were of losing. They gave up the figure-skating style that Del favoured and came out forechecking like demons. Onion Head, suffering from hurt feelings, began dealing out vicious hip checks at centre ice. Raccoon Coogle threw away the leg brace and went on a scoring spree. T-Bar Kelly wanted to be loved more than anything. When Wolf growled in his face, he got tunnel vision. The result was that the Northfield Comets went on a six-game winning streak. The whole town picked up. Orville was thinking about making a banner of the new slogan so they could display it on the bus. Del thought maybe they should wait and see how things went. Wolf was back to normal, barking at the referees, stalking behind the bench like a zoo animal. T-Bar was stopping everything as if he had radar. Deep down inside T-Bar knew his luck had changed because of the four-leaf clover he glued inside his right skate.

"Hello, Del, this is Aubrey Shanks. What the hell is going down in Northfield?"

Del held the phone out and let Shanks talk to the empty room. He knew Shanks was out of joint because the Comets were winning.

"I don't know what you're talking about," Del answered.

"The hell you don't." Shanks was in a fury. "That moron Wolf Slawson threw a garbage can on the ice last night in Youngstown. Dumped it all over the linesman."

Del inquired cautiously, "Did the referee send in a report?"

"You know bloody well he didn't. First of all, he was afraid of Slawson and, second of all, you boys from Northfield smoothed him over after the game."

Del said, "Oops, I've got a customer." He left the receiver dangling with Shanks' ugly voice rasping in the rafters.

The Comets finished the regular season with 15 wins, eight losses and three ties. Their hopeless season had turned around. They easily qualified for the playoffs. In the first round of the playoffs, they eliminated the Fairweather Honkers from post-season play by taking the best-of-three in two games. In the second round against Lovely Lake, they were forced to win the third and deciding game in overtime. All that stood between them and the Wheatland Cup was a three-game series with the Bluffsville Blades. What was most galling to League Commissioner Shanks was that the Comets had earned the extra home game. Del and Orville had stopped talking to Shanks on the telephone. They knew that Wolf Slawson's methods had worked without degenerating too far into goon hockey. If things went right, the playoffs would remain without incident, at least until the final game. Once it came down to one shot for all the marbles, Wolf might become an uncontrollable beast.

His value as coach was the inspirational fear he raised in his own team and the terror his unpredictability caused in the opposition. Wolf liked to snack on sardines right out of the tin in the dressing room so he could burp fish breath into the referee's face when he skated over to the Northfield bench.

The Comets had a tradition. On game days against the Bluffsville Blades, the bus left Northfield at 3 in the afternoon. That way the team could stop halfway and have a pre-game meal together at Granny's Diner in Lonesome. Some of the players refrained from eating. T-Bar and Onion Head always had the dumplings with chicken liver gravy. The Bluffsville Blades also stopped at Granny's on their way into Northfield on game nights. It was as if both teams needed to gather strength before entering enemy territory. After the game was over, the visitors' bus would usually pull out and head for the Lonesome Hotel bar to avoid ugly incidents.

Orville nudged Del in the ribs at the end of the second period of the first playoff game. "Granny must be servin' some heavy food." The Comets playing at home had built up a 4-0 lead.

Dwayne Semple was firing BBs from the point. They got in trouble in the third period when T-Bar started playing goal for the crowd instead of the team. His showboating resulted in two quick tallies at the 10-minute mark. Then he juggled a long shot in the last minute. It dropped over his shoulder into the net. Wolf sent out five defencemen to kill off the final seconds. He instructed Onion Head to tell T-Bar if he let in another goal, he would have his balls for a necktie.

Game 2 in Bluffsville was a different story. Several fights broke out in the crowd before the puck was dropped. Spit was raining down from overhead bleachers. During the first shift, number 4 for the Blades, Boris Fistic, speared Dwayne Semple as he shifted the puck travelling through centre ice. Semple went down like a pole-axed steer and was carried off to the dressing room. Onion Head attacked Fistic and picked up the extra two minutes for being the instigator. On his way to the penalty box, he started a fight with Bronco Provotski that got them both thrown out. The fans in Bluffsville were throwing pennies and the odd battery. Wolf was crouching on top of the boards like a snarling Doberman looking for a chance to leap onto the referee. When the smoke cleared, the Comets were down 2-0. When his penalty was up, Fistic went to his own bench and never left it for the duration of the game. Wolf began heckling Eagle Perkins, the Bluffsville coach, demanding that he put number 4 back on the ice. Eagle held his nose and made chicken sounds which drove Wolf into spasms of rage.

By the third period, the game was lost. Bluffsville had a good power play. They filled the net in answer to Wolf's desire for revenge. The final score was Bluffsville 7, Northfield 3. Now T-Bar Kelly was a flake but not without reasons. When he saw Dwayne leave the game, he knew that winning was in doubt. When Wolf attacked his pads between periods with a hockey stick, T-Bar began to get tunnel vision. Every goal he let in burned in him like a hot poker. When the final buzzer sounded, and after the obligatory pushing and shoving, T-Bar slowly skated along the boards. He timed his arrival at the exit to coincide with that of Bluffsville's number 4. Inspired by some ungodly vision, he lifted his stick like a double-bladed axe and brought it down on Fistic's back. It took the Comets three hours to disentangle themselves from the brawl that ensued. Wolf chased Eagle Perkins two miles across a frozen Hutterite field before he gave up and trotted back to the bus. The Northfield Comets and their fans stopped at the Lonesome Hotel on their way home. It was a mistake because two dozen hard-core Bluffsville supporters following in vehicles rushed in and started another donnybrook.

The phone rang at 7 a.m. "Hello, that you, Del? Are you up?"

"Dammit, you know it, Shanks. I open up the store at 7:30."

Aubrey Shanks had waited up all night to make this call. His voice was as thick as George's coffee. "Just want you to know that gawdamn goofball hippie goalie of yours is suspended for the balance of the season for that unprovoked attack."

"Aubrey, aren't you being a little hasty. There was fault on both sides."

"Listen to me, Del," snorted Shanks. "He's suspended. Now you've appealed and it ain't successful. So now you can live or die with Slim in the final game. Ha, ha. Good luck, your whole town is full of bumheads and dumbsticks."

Later in the morning Del wandered over to the coffee shop. "Must have been quite a game," George remarked while cleaning off the table. Del filled the folks in on his conversation with Shanks.

Orville bounced his belly against the table. "That SOB is going to pay for insulting the good folks of Northfield."

Del winced. "No time for a political speech. I guess we'll have to go with Slim in the nets next Friday night."

Orville lifted his eyebrows. "May as well mail Bluffsville the two points." Problem was, after the brawl in Lonesome, Slim just disappeared into thin air. Wolf drove around town looking for him in the usual places. Finally, Slim's cousin Henry told Wolf that Slim had been called up to Edmonton to start a new job.

"He's sorry he won't be able to play in the big game."

Slim never had a job in his life. Henry was lucky Wolf was troubled by a hangover or he might have had his throat ripped out for being the bearer of bad news. Del got on the phone to try to reason with Shanks. "Aubrey, we've been in this league a long time. These incidents have a way of being blown into full-scale misunderstandings."

Shanks was eating a piece of Mrs. Shanks' Boston cream pie while he conversed with Del. He smacked his lips at the end of his own sentences and swallowed when Del tried to speak. "That hippie dink goalie is out and that's that. But since Slim is out of town, I'll give you a break."

Del was waiting for this opportunity. "What kind of a break?"

Shanks crooned back into the phone: "It wouldn't be fair to Bluffsville if you filled in with a ringer. But you can add to your roster any goalie who has ever been on it in the past."

Orville and Del were back sitting at George's along with Wolf and some of the players. They were scanning the roster lists for the past 20 years looking for a goalie.

"Maybe we can get Tiny Simpson," offered Onion Head.

Orville looked up. "Tiny had his leg amputated last year."

George remembered, "About five years ago there was a decent guy in the nets."

"Yeah, Chester Stonewall, but he's working on the oil rigs off Sable Island," Del replied.

Smudge Peabody had been sitting in the corner reading his newspaper. "Don't mind me my two bits' worth but seems the town's got a big problem. Now there was only one goalie ever worth anything in Northfield. The one and only Dutch Mowbray. Why, he played six games for the Detroit Red Wings in '53 and all those years in the minor pro leagues."

Orville had come back from squeezing himself through the washroom door. "Dutch was a fine goalie in his day but he was almost collecting his pension when he sat all those years behind Sawchuk."

Del looked up from the lists. "The only thing about it is that he qualifies because he played for the town from '67 through '69."

Smudge peered through the smoky room and said, "It's just like riding a bicycle. You never forget. Let's go out and talk to him."

Dutch Mowbray was changing the oil in his tractor when Orville, Del and Smudge turned up at his barn door. "How you boys doin'? What can I do for you?" He stood before them in greasy overalls with a dark oil stain running through his yellowing white hair. On the bridge of his nose were the heaviest pair of glasses ever constructed.

Orville stuck his authority out. "We was just wondering if you ever hanker to get back in the nets."

"No, can't say that I miss it much," Dutch answered.

Del asked, "Guess there's a lot of pressure playing in the nets and of course with your eyesight being bad and all that it would be risky?"

Dutch put down his oily rag. "I'll tell you boys a little secret. I was successful because of my bad eyes."

"You don't say," Smudge offered.

"I never bothered looking at the puck. I played the angles. I figured out where it was going by reflex rather than eyesight. In fact, I couldn't even see the puck when it was outside the blue line. It used to make me damn mad when I saw the little devil close up because that meant it was behind me. I loved the game but hated the practising."

Coming out from the barn into natural light, Del noticed the scars and dents that were magnified in Dutch's face, giving his lips a puckered look. Dutch went on. "Gave my pads away in '71 to the Simpson kid."

Del had just finished getting rid of Thelma Birtles and her six kids who were running up and down his store's walls. The door chimes sounded and in walked Commissioner Aubrey Shanks.

"I heard a rumour that you birds are thinking about putting Dutch Mowbray in the nets on Friday night."

Del snapped back, "What if we are?"

"The league won't allow it on the grounds that he's a geriatric who might get hisself killed."

Del opened the desk drawer and pulled out his pile of ancient Northfield rosters. "Here it is, Shanks, in black and white. Mowbray, Dutch, goalie '66 to '69. Now you get out of town before Wolf Slawson finds out you're here and turns your ugly buttocks into dog food."

On Wednesday night Orville and Del sat disconsolate in the Northfield Hotel beer parlour. "The biggest game of the year and we've got a 73-year-old blind goalie." Del lifted his hand and waved for another round. Orville ordered two pickled eggs. Just when depression was getting the best of them, in swaggered Smudge Peabody.

"What you boys looking so down in the mouth about?" Smudge asked.

Del answered, "It's like this, Smudge, we're worried that Dutch is liable to end up in a pine box on Friday night."

Smudge winked. "Won't happen if you don't let it happen."

"How's that?"

"I drove over to Lonesome and had supper at Granny's this evening. Not many people in there. Yesterday, Aubrey Shanks and Eagle Perkins came in to plan the Friday night team dinner. Since Dutch'll be in the nets, they think the game is a foregone conclusion. They're planning on leaving Bluffsville early so they can have a fully catered team meal at Granny's before they move on to Northfield. Then a big bash later on after the game at the Lonesome Hotel."

Del looked a little green. "That's confidence for you."

"What do you mean, if we don't let it happen?" wondered Orville.

"I mean just that," snickered Smudge. "We have an old man with grit in goal but we need a bit of an edge. I chatted up Granny. She told me she gets Diane at the Northfield Bakery to supply her desserts. Now everybody knows that young Rose works all night at the bakery. Granny told me she ordered 25 Nanaimo bars for Friday night."

Two a.m. Friday, Orville and Del pulled up in front of the Northfield Bakery in Orville's Crown Victoria. They could see Rose through the foggy picture window. Orville tapped on the glass with his car keys. Soon Rose's face appeared and she went around and opened the door.

"What are you two doing here?"

Orville laughed and said, "We was going home from the bar. We thought we'd drop by and get a snack."

"Come on in, I've got some coffee brewing in the back."

Orville and Del sipped coffee and munched on ginger snaps.

"What's in the big mixer?"

"Oh, just the ingredients for a batch of Nanaimo bars."

"That so," said Del. "Quite a piece of machinery. Mind if I have a closer look?"

Half an hour later, Orville and Del bid Rose good night.

"Well?" Orville asked impatiently. "How much did you manage to add?"

Del smiled. "I decided to go all the way. I threw in all five packages of Ex-Lax."

"No!"

"If you're gonna do something, you may as well go all the way. Besides, only half of 'em will eat dessert. That's all we need."

Orville beamed. "That Rose is a swell baker."

Del laughed. "Hear she makes a hell of a Nanaimo bar."

There was a lot of movement off the bus when the Bluffsville Blades arrived at the Northfield rink. The Northfield fans were already gathering in front of the building. Some of them were screaming threats at the beleaguered Blades. Smudge was taking tickets at the main door.

"Good evening, boys, Eagle. How's it hanging, Aubrey?" Smudge was in his element searching their faces for a sign of weakness. Aubrey was carrying his dessert in a brown paper bag.

Eagle puffed himself up. "Had a good dinner and team meeting at Granny's, we're gonna be loose tonight!"

T-Bar was in the Northfield dressing room helping Dutch Mowbray put on his hockey gear. Dutch stood there looking like an old tom turkey in his long johns. Wolf was bouncing off the walls telling his defencemen to play it tight and his forwards to shoot the bloody puck.

"We have a pro in goal tonight. Let's not leave them on his doorstep."

Dutch finally got into his pads and put on his thick horn-rimmed glasses. T-Bar was adjusting the straps on the goalie mask. Dutch looked at him. "Never wore one, never will. Damn things only block yer vision."

Del, standing behind Dutch, said, "What the hell you talking about? Last Monday you told us you was blind. What difference will it make? Put the damn mask on and save your life."

"Never has, never will. End of subject."

Del went over to Wolf to plead with him to talk Dutch into the mask. Wolf was already wearing his game face. He growled at Del and told him without words to get out of his room. Dutch reached out and put something in Del's hand.

"Take good care of 'em. Mr. Adams bought 'em for me in '55." Del was holding a full set of dentures.

During the pre-game skate, Dutch worked, scraping back and forth in the crease as if looking for some kind of miracle of traction. He stood nonchalantly facing shots from the point. When Dwayne whistled a puck by his ear, he crossed himself and tucked his head further into his shoulders.

Onion Head skated over to him. "Do you want me to block the shot or would you rather see it all the way?"

Dutch impatiently slapped his stick on the ice. "I don't exactly see the puck, I feel the shooter's motion."

In the lobby, Aubrey was making jokes to Del and Orville.

"I suppose you fellows pumped that old dude full of Geritol, huh? Hope he doesn't fall asleep in the middle of the game."

After that comment, he unwrapped his Nanaimo bar and washed it down with a cup of rink java.

"I'm willing to put a little wager down on our boys tonight," Orville said.
"That so. How about a hundred bucks?"
"You're on."
The players went back into the dressing room while the Zamboni prepared the ice for the faceoff. Wolf was snarling at his defencemen.
"If anybody goes one-on-one with Dutch, I'll be waiting here at the gate with my switchblade and you'll be singing falsetto. Remember, dump, chase and staple. No fightin' till the third period and then only if we're out of it." Wolf began to pound his chest and howl like a wolf at the moon.

The Northfield Comets came out of the dressing room like a pack of wolves. When they hit the ice, the crowd went crazy. Dutch came out last and skated down to the wrong end of the rink. Onion Head, wielding his stick like a scythe among the black-clad Blades, went down and retrieved him. Orville and Del, sitting in the poop deck over the south end, were watching the Bluffsville bench. Only about six of their players had come onto the ice; a few more were sitting with their heads down on the bench.

Aubrey was looking pretty shaky. "I'm feeling a little attack. Just going to hit the men's room before the action starts."

In the first minute, a puck deflected off a Comet player at centre ice and ticked onto Bronco Provotski's stick, giving him a clear breakaway. He cruised in on Dutch, deking with his shoulders and his head. Dutch stayed motionless at the top of the crease. When Bronco veered across the front of the net to the backhand, Dutch stayed on his feet. Suddenly his goalie stick recoiled like a cobra and he poke-checked the puck off of Bronco's stick. By the time Aubrey returned from the john, the Comets, possessed by lupine tenacity, were swarming around the Bluffsville net. The score was already 2-0. In the rest of the period, Dutch faced only a long slapshot that hit him in the shoulder and ricocheted over the glass. Eagle Perkins had left the bench and gone back into the dressing room. Aubrey was no sooner sitting than he excused himself and went back for more. Orville and Del were living it up, cheering wildly.

"Good thing they're wearing their black uniforms," quipped Orville.

The Bluffsville bench could hardy manage a line change. When Aubrey appeared again, the score was 5-0. Bluffsville had iced the puck 25 times.

In the first intermission, Dutch asked Onion Head, "Did that puck hit me?" "No, that was the evening freight that ran into you. Didn't you see it coming down the track?"

Out in the lobby, the crowd was pounding on the can door telling Aubrey to hurry up. He'd stagger out the door and go quickly to the end of the line. "What's wrong, Shanks?" asked Smudge.

"Don't rightly know. I'm a touch under the weather."

Smudge offered Aubrey a Player's Filter.

"No thanks, Smudge, I'm feeling a little peculiar."

"You know, Aubrey, there's a real bad bout of influenza going around these days. Looks like you and your Bluffsville boys have caught it."

Aubrey was soon back in riding the porcelain bronco.

Meanwhile, Wolf, smelling blood, was going crazy in the dressing room. "Now is the time to hit everything that moves out there. Kill the body, the head dies."

The Comets came out hitting in the second period. Even when they were short-handed, they controlled the play. Dwayne Semple, ragging the puck, saw an opening and headed straight for the Bluffsville net. Before he got there, the Bluffsville goalie was headed to the bench.

"Easiest goal I ever scored," he said later in the bar.

Dutch, playing the angles, stopped a half-dozen shots, sweeping the puck into the corners.

Wolf was screaming, "Kill number 4."

Boris Fistic was skating on his ankles, using his stick like a rudder to help him navigate in his own end. Wolf grabbed Onion Head at the bench and asked him why he wouldn't go in deep and nail Boris.

"Jeezuz, Wolf, get off my back, that guy smells like a septic tank."

By the third period, Aubrey Shanks was walking as if he had the world's worst case of ring of fire. Eagle Perkins and the Bluffsville trainer were holding on to each other in the throes of gastric distress.

Smudge slapped Aubrey Shanks a little roughly on the shoulder and said, "Honestly, Aubrey, your boys are skating tonight like they're carrying a load of lead in their pants."

Aubrey was in no position to argue. He opened his wallet and paid Orville the hundred dollars. Orville sent Del down behind the bench to tell Wolf that there was no need for a riot tonight.

"Wolf, those Blades are spent. Let 'em out of here with their lives."

Wolf was still whining and shaking. Pleading for somebody, anybody, to get even with Boris.

Aubrey presented the fabled Wheatland Cup to Del and Wolf and Dwayne in the world's shortest-ever formal presentation. He quickly excused himself and headed for the men's room. It was a long time before the Bluffsville Blades were able to crawl out of the dressing room to the safety of the bus. The rink lights had been turned off for half an hour. Wolf Slawson had stayed outside the building howling like a madman, screaming at number 4 to come out and face the music. When he gave up and went to the celebration at the Northfield Hotel, the Bluffsville team made its exit.

In the bar, Onion Head stood up and made the toast:

"This win is for Dutch. Old and blind he may be, he never lost his touch."

## Gordie's Floral Sky
*Don Kerr*

this wide blue sky's the rink
gordie as a kid practised hockey on
skates slicing jet rails
stickhandling in and out
of clouds like jam cans frozen
in the blue ice or slop pails the Bentleys
deked round over the river in Delisle.

gordie at Floral
flashing down the thin road
spraying long swirls of cirrus
speeds over the blue line of the horizon
on the long skate to Detroit   Chicago   Toronto   New York

my old man used to sit in his car at the airport
to watch those sky games   he was a great sports fan
and liked a good seat at a good price

the game's in its dying minutes and the clouds
turn violet with applause   red lake and ochre
and hey they say   hey gordie
hey max   hey doug   hey roy
net that big fat harvest moon

dent the twine
ignite that red light
the dying sun
skate that 100% Canadian content sky
same as when you were a kid gordie
skating the school rink as night came on
and you heard the cheers coming down the road
gathering you up in the embrace
of a goalmouth scramble
a western sky

## Gordie Howe Statue, Saskatoon
*Myrna Garanis*

East of the Vietnamese Bakery, fenced off from other
forwards, Gordie Howe cemented to a pedestal,
in perpetual scoring stance. Metal stick, metal gloves,
elbows sharp-edged as always.

You'd pass him on the way to St. Paul's, a hospital
only hookers wandered round at night. Riversdale
no longer in its heyday, bowed down by pawn shops,
bingo and steel-barred doors. Gordie would zing
occasional slapshots their way if he could.
His eyes are fixed on the smooth straight sheet ahead,
puck poised for drilling pimps between the eyes.
Check the angle of his skates barely clinging
to that platform.

When the lease is up, city council's set to move him
out of there. But where is his rightful place? Where
does an aged player head after Avenue A and 20th Street,
a man turning to stone himself, staring at the knuckles.

## The Woman Behind the Mask
*Calvin Daniels*

Terry Chamberlin sat in the dressing room, the sweat dripping from his nose, intermittently plopping onto his hair-covered chest. He had managed to pull off his sweater and top gear, but his legs were still encased in thick leather pads, his feet unseen inside skates, the energy to go further in the undressing process seemingly sucked from his body.

"Tough game, eh, Terry?" said a voice.

Chamberlin shook his head slightly as if waking from a dream. He looked across the room. The voice belonged to George Kerr, the sports reporter with the *Parkland Review*. Kerr was a pretty good writer. Chamberlin thought he should be working with a daily in the city, but since his wife was head nurse at the hospital, he simply couldn't move and risk losing her fat salary.

"Guess so. Just when I think things are going my way..." There was a silence before Chamberlin continued. "I still can't believe I missed that knuckleball floater from the blue line. My God, a peewee can stop those."

"Everybody has an off game," offered Kerr.

"But most people have an on game once in a while. No wonder I sit on the end of the bench until the lousy teams come to town. Then I blow those games too."

Thirty years old and buried in a minor league so far from the NHL it wasn't even a dream anymore, Chamberlin wondered why he still cared. He should be out getting a real job instead of worrying about a $500-a-game hockey career, but there was still a chance the American Hockey League, or some European team, might take a chance if he could put together one good season.

"You've got to relax. You play like you're waiting for the mistake to happen." Kerr's words brought him back to the present.

"It usually does."

"Maybe you need an edge," suggested Kerr.

"If you're going to suggest drugs—"

"Come on, you know me better than that, Terry," interrupted Kerr. "No, I'm thinking of something more psychological."

"I'm surprised you know the word," Chamberlin said with a weak smile.

"I study my *Funk & Wagnalls*," Kerr smiled back.

"So what's this idea of yours?"

"I know this woman who paints goaltender masks. Some of the guys that have gone to her suggest the masks make them better. Change their perspective. Maybe all you need is a fresh start."

"As crazy as that sounds, I might go see her. Besides, if I don't do something soon, the coach is going to kick my butt back to life as a civilian," and despite the long bus rides, the greasy post-game hamburgers and the always-sore muscles, Chamberlin knew he feared civilian life.

Hockey was all he really knew, having given up on university for a shot at the pros. He hadn't made it, although he had been fighting to climb his way to one more shot for more than a decade.

"What's her name?" he asked.

"Michelle Brunsell."

★★★

Chamberlin pulled his Chrysler into the driveway at 103 Bradbrooke Avenue.

He double-checked the address scrawled on a piece of paper just to be sure. He shut off the car and grabbed the goaltender's helmet that had occupied the passenger seat on the trip across town.

Nice place, he thought as he walked the short brick path to the front door. He climbed the three steps and reached for the doorbell. Before he could press it, the door opened.

"Come in," said a woman.

Chamberlin was a little surprised.

"You must be Terry Chamberlin," said the woman. She was about five foot six, thin, with long black hair and dark eyes. She was wearing a dark purple sweater and rather tight jeans. Although a little thinner than the women Chamberlin was normally attracted to, he still couldn't help a quick once-over with his eyes and a smile.

"And you are Miss Brunsell?"

"Oh, please, call me Michelle."

"All right."

"Well, let's go sit down and find out exactly what we can do for each other," she said. "Please come this way."

It was a moderately furnished living room, with a brown patterned chesterfield and chair, and a glass-topped coffee table. In its centre was a stained glass bowl held on three legs by what appeared to be some sort of Egyptian god.

"I have a taste for the unusual," the woman said, in response to Chamberlin's stare. "I guess that's why I started painting helmets."

"Well, George Kerr says you might be able to do something with mine," he said, holding it up for her to see.

"So what did you have in mind?" she asked, placing the helmet on the table. "Can I get you a cup of herbal tea?"

Chamberlin shook his head. "I have no idea. I've been playing poorly and George suggested a painted helmet might help me turn things around. Frankly, I'm not convinced, but I'll try anything at this point. I just hope it helps."

"That's up to you," she said. "So what do you want on this?"

"Well, I play for the Cougars. Maybe something like a cougar's head."

"Perhaps. The cougar is an animal of cunning and quickness. Those are attributes a goaltender must have, are they not?"

"I suppose," he said, his brow furrowing slightly.

"You may indeed have the spirits that will allow me to create one of the special helmets."

"Excuse me, but you're losing me here."

"Of course. Please sit down," she said, offering Chamberlin a chair. "It will become clear soon enough. So tell me, when were you born?"

"April 12."

"Aries the ram. Power and determination. That is good. I will create a helmet for you, and it will help you play better. It will be the embodiment of the skills you need. You will be inspired by it. You will draw from it."

"Look, Miss Brunsell—"

"Michelle."

"This is sounding pretty weird."

"Oh excuse me. We artists are a bit strange, I guess. Sometimes we take our work a little too seriously." Her face broke into a smile. "I'll tell you what, leave the helmet with me today and I'll think about a design. Stop back tomorrow evening."

"I suppose it's worth a shot. There's a day off in the schedule and I can use my spare helmet for practice."

"Good. Then I'll see you tomorrow."

★★★

The next morning Chamberlin had to dig deep in his locker to find the old goaltender's helmet. He hadn't worn it for over a season, but it made it through the day's practice.

"Where's your regular?" a voice asked from across the room.

The voice belonged to Art Belanger, the team's gnarled equipment manager. He was the only one in the room, the others either dressed and gone, or still enjoying the post-practice shower. Belanger was busily picking up sweat-soaked towels and gear and tossing them into a cart.

"It's being painted."

"Going fancy on us, are you?" said Belanger, his smile revealing three rotted teeth.

"Michelle says she'll do a good job."

"You didn't take it to Michelle Brunsell, did you?"

"Yeah. You know her?"

"Let's say we've met. I had her paint a mask for old-timers hockey once."

"Did it do any good?"

"Huh!"

"I mean did it look good?" asked Chamberlin, reaching down to loosen the buckles on the back of his pads.

"Let's just say it didn't turn out the way I expected."

"What the hell does that mean?" he asked, reaching for the last buckle with a groan.

"I just wanted a painted mask, but, well, this is going to sound weird, but I played better. It was like the mask gave me energy ... oh, I don't know."

Looking up, Chamberlin saw that Belanger was quite pale, his eyes reflecting a mind deep in thought. There was more to this than Belanger was letting on, but he did say he played better. That was the bottom line, to play the game the way he had always dreamed but never quite had the skill to achieve.

Chamberlin rose from the floor, grabbed his towel off the bench and headed for the shower.

"Thanks," he said, nodding at Belanger.

"You may not say that one day," He heard Belanger whisper as he stepped into the steam-filled room.

★★★

Chamberlin couldn't help but wonder what Michelle had designed for him as he drove to her home the next day. There was hope in the thought that maybe the simple helmet would make the difference.

But there was also Belanger's veiled warnings swimming in and out of his consciousness, threatening his dream.

Chamberlin was unsure exactly what this woman was offering him. She talked in riddles, wrapped in a sort of mysticism, but perhaps that was the secret. If he believed in her ability, the ability of the mask, then it would come true. He had read that the mind had powers few ever truly mastered. It had the ability to do far more than to be a storehouse and retrieval system for fact and minutiae.

Chamberlin pulled the car into the driveway and was again met at the door before he had time to ring the doorbell.

"Oh, Terry, come in," said Michelle, this time wearing a long dark purple dress.

"Thank you."

"I think I have this figured out," she offered as she led him down the hallway, this time pausing in front of the door at the hall's end. She lifted a key from a delicate chain around her neck and opened the door.

The room was lit only by candles. It was small. A combination desk/workbench occupied a large portion of the floor space. On the corner of the desk there was a pile of papers, some with crude designs, others with more elaborate drawings. An easel on a joint-armed pivot was pushed to one side above the desk. Next to it was a small shelf cluttered with bottles and tubes of paint and brushes. There was a chair behind the desk and one along the wall.

The helmet sat in the middle of five burning candles in the centre of the desk.

"Most clients think it's a little strange," she replied with a smile.

Chamberlin looked around the room. The walls were adorned with pictures of painted helmets. Some he recognized as those of rival players, and each had an individuality to it.

"See anything you like?"

"They're all great," said Chamberlin.

"Some are just paint jobs, but others, well, they turned out better, shall we say. I think I can do something special for you," she said.

"That sounds good, what do you have in mind?"

"Remember what I said about drawing on the attributes of the cougar and the ram. Well, that was more than just talk. If you're willing, I can turn things around for you."

"Okay, Michelle, you're starting to talk a lot of strange stuff again. All I came here for was to get my helmet painted, and only because Kerr said it might help."

"It will."

"How can you be so sure? What do you mean, draw from it?" At this point, he was starting to think this woman was as daft as the idea had been when George first suggested it.

It had always been a case of him being just good enough to make the team, but never good enough to be the star. He had made the midget team in town only because he and Tony Kohlert were the only goaltenders in the age range. Tony had played 42 of 50 games that season.

Now it was more of the same. By the time senior hockey rolled into most players' careers, they had decided the risk of injury and the need to punch a clock necessitated retirement. But he had kept playing the game, again largely because he and Frank Burns were the only guys willing to face flying frozen rubber every other night. Actually, that wasn't true either. Frank faced most of the rubber, while he warmed the seat at the end of the bench.

Just once he would like to be the guy the coach relied on in big games, instead of being the guy inserted into the lineup only against teams the Cougars could easily handle. Even then, the coach seemed reluctant, but Burns needed a night off once in a while.

"Does it matter how I know? Isn't it enough that it will work?"

"You're right. So what will this cost?"

"Money is not paramount at this time. We will discuss a fee in the future."

"Okay, so what's next?"

"You must do as I ask," said Michelle. "I have most of the things that I need," she added, walking over to the desk and bringing out a copper bowl from a drawer. "There are the whiskers of the cougar, and flakes from the horn of a ram ..."

"What the hell are you talking about?"

"These things are needed. They will be distilled and mixed with the paints I use. They will allow you to draw directly on the powers these animals possess."

Chamberlin found himself taking a step toward the closed door. He wanted to win, but this woman was obviously lost in another world. Talk of boosting his inner confidence was one thing, but distilling the whiskers of a cat? They put people in small padded cells for that.

"You are unsure, Chamberlin? That is to be expected. Most of us live in a world where we fear and condemn what we do not understand. Yet in that we find our weakness. There is a common thread running through the existence of each plant and animal in this world. It extends across the world and flows through time and space. If we can accept the reality of the commonality that is integral to each of us, we can draw on others within the continuum when it is required. In your case, you already have ties to the ram through astrology and the cougar through your team. These things may appear random, but they are not. They are connected just as time and space are. All I wish to do is allow you to draw on the reality which already exists."

Chamberlin was not sure why he stood there. Part of him wanted to turn and run from this woman talking concepts which seemed mere gibberish, but another part implored him to stay. It was as if in the back of his mind, deep within its unused mysteries, a tiny voice was screaming that this woman was not a crackpot. Instead, she was simply able to see beyond the confines in which humans had for centuries bound themselves.

"I should leave," he said.

"But then you will not fulfill your dream."

Chamberlin felt his head drop. She was right. She might be talking nonsense, or reciting the secret of existence, but either way it was his only chance at his time in the limelight.

"So what must I do?"

Michelle took the bowl and placed it on a small stand. She then placed a group of five coloured candles under it. From a bottle, she added what appeared to be water, and then powders from three pouches.

"Come over here," she ordered.

Slowly, Chamberlin complied. He was now standing beside the woman. She raised the knife and drew its blade smoothly across his palm. There was no pain, and his blood began to drip into the bowl, soon becoming a steady trickle.

Next she closed the hand, holding it for a few seconds before letting it go. Chamberlin stepped back, shaking his head slightly from side to side as if coming out of a fog.

He opened his hand, holding it close to his face. There was no blood. No cut. No scar.

Chamberlin wanted to ask what was happening, but he couldn't find the words in the fog that still engulfed his mind. No, it wasn't a mind-created haze. It seemed to come from the steam rising from the bowl, now glowing a bright crimson — the blood, his blood, merging with the melting horn, whiskers and herbs. Within the steam, Chamberlin could see the cougars stalking prey, rams butting heads, himself stopping hockey pucks, the images seeming to merge as the components in the bowl had done.

Brunsell took the bowl and carefully poured its contents into several small vials of paint of various hues. Once finished, she took a small, thin wand and stirred the concoction. She then sat at the table and began to paint.

Chamberlin was unsure how long it took to create the mask. He simply stood there watching as the alluring woman with the strange philosophies drew the image of a goaltender stopping a breakaway. Within the gloved hand, there was just a ghost image of a snarling cougar, and within the pads the faint outline of a ram.

"There! It is complete," she said, finally turning to speak to Chamberlin. "Do you like it?"

"I still don't understand all that happened here."

"To understand is not important. To accept is the only thing that matters."

★★★

Fate played its hand the next night. The Tofield Timberwolves were in town. They were leading the league and were on an extended winning streak. Chamberlin showed up at the rink, knowing he would be riding the pines— until Burns appeared with a fever of 100 degrees. Reluctantly, the coach turned to Chamberlin.

Chamberlin was not sure whether the energies Brunsell had spoken of included butterflies, but there were certainly enough of them churning in his stomach during warm-ups, and more than a few easy shots were still finding the twine.

"Think the fancy mask is going to help?" asked Terry Norris with a laugh. Norris was the leading scorer on the Timberwolves, and Chamberlin shuddered at his words. *I just hope the defence is on tonight*, he thought as the puck was dropped at centre ice.

Ten minutes in, he learned it was not. Norris blew around the left defenceman and barrelled down on the goaltender. The butterflies returned as Chamberlin felt himself going down, suckered by a deke right. Norris pulled the puck back to the left and went high on the glove side.

The crowd went wild. Chamberlin looked up to see Norris skating away shaking his head. *It must have gone over the net*, he thought.

"Can I have the puck?" asked a linesman, skating in from the left.

"What?"

"The puck. In your glove," he said, pointing at Chamberlin's mitt with a whistle-adorned finger. Chamberlin looked at the glove. He opened it slowly. There was the puck, all right. Yet he had not felt the shot, could not remember the move to make the catch.

Chamberlin tossed the puck to the man in stripes and smiled. Maybe Brunsell knew something after all.

★★★

For the next six weeks, it was Burns who rode the bench. Chamberlin had shut out the Timberwolves that night and since had lost only two games, one of those in overtime.

It was what he had always wanted. It was now Chamberlin whom Kerr ferreted out most nights for a comment on the game. In one story Kerr had even suggested it was catlike reflexes that was allowing Chamberlin to shine. It had been weeks since he had bought himself a cup of coffee, thanks to the generosity of appreciative fans. There was even an offer to play for an all-star senior team planning a tour of Europe in the spring.

Whatever Brunsell had done, it was working.

"I guess you were worried for nothing, eh?" He told Belanger one night, after stonewalling the rival Wheat Kings 4-1.

"Don't be too quick with your assumptions," the old equipment man said as he stopped sweeping the dressing room floor. "Have you paid for the mask yet?"

In spite of the weeks that had passed, the answer was no, yet he had never even thought of returning to Michelle's to settle the account. It was strange, because he always paid his bills.

"So I haven't paid. I will."

"Yes, you will, my friend, and the price may be higher than you think."

"What does that mean?" asked Chamberlin.

"How old do you think I am?"

"What does that have to do with anything?"

"How old?" Belanger asked again in a stronger tone.

"Oh, maybe 50, 60."

"Try 41."

"You're kidding," said Chamberlin, leaning back against the lockers. Belanger's hair was almost white, and thin on top. Deep lines were already etched in the man's forehead. The hands that clasped the broom were weathered and thin. There was a stoop to his walk.

"I wish I was. You know how the life energies of all things are connected? How you draw on the energies of others to play so well?"

"I don't understand, but it works."

"Well, it works both ways. Somehow Brunsell draws on the energies of those she paints for. We age and she does not. Every time you win, she drains weeks of life from you to feed her eternal youth."

Chamberlin ran his fingers through his hair. He had noticed a few white strands recently but figured it was just a natural thing. Now here was Belanger suggesting Brunsell was sucking his life essence away to feed her own youth. Two months ago, he would have thought Belanger was crazy, but now after wearing the mask?

"What can I do?"

"Give up the mask."

"And go back to the bench. That's some choice," he said as he walked slowly from the room.

The playoffs were only a week away and the team was relying on Chamberlin backstopping them to a win over the Timberwolves, but perhaps the cost was too high, he thought.

That night, against the lowly Renegades, Chamberlin left the painted mask in his locker, instead donning his old helmet. The Renegades won 6-4.

"Tough game," said Kerr, a notepad in one hand, a pen poised to write in the other.

"We all have 'em."

"I noticed you weren't wearing the fancy mask."

"There was a screw missing and we didn't have a spare," said Chamberlin.

The next night he was back in net, again without the painted mask. It was another loss. Two more and it was Burns back in the net.

"You made the right decision," Belanger assured him after Chamberlin's benching. "It may not seem like it, but it is."

Burns was rusty after his tenure on the bench, and with the playoffs underway, things did not look good for the Cougars. In the first game they lost a heartbreaker 5-4, and found themselves blown out in the second.

"It could be a short series," said Kerr after the second game. "Too bad your game went sour."

"Yeah," he said, glancing up at the painted mask sitting on the shelf in his locker.

Chamberlin sat in the dressing room long after the other players had showered and gone. He knew if he put the mask back on, he would never be able to give it up again. He also knew he could beat the Timberwolves by drawing on the mask's power. He could be an aging hero or he could just ride the bench to nowhere.

Slowly, he rose and left the dressing room, walking down the hallways to the concession area.

Chamberlin was surprised when he saw Michelle standing near the door.

"Hello, Terry," she said with a smile, as she moved into a position between the door and Chamberlin.

"What are you doing here?"

"I understand Belanger has been telling tales," she said.

Chamberlin was not sure how to respond. There was an awkward silence.

"Come now, you really don't believe his stories, do you?"

"He said you once painted a mask for him."

"Yes."

"Did it give him the power?"

"For a while it did, but then he ruined it."

"What do you mean?"

"The power wasn't enough for him. He started betting on games he played in. He was drawing on the power of others to line his pockets. The power took care of things."

Brunsell was no longer looking at Chamberlin but was instead staring at a point somewhere beyond his left shoulder. He twisted his head in time to see Belanger, ashen-faced, staring at Brunsell.

"The power is pure. Do not abuse it," she said, turning to leave.

"Then what do I owe you?"

"In time," she said as the door closed behind her.

★★★

The next day there was a noticeable hush as Chamberlin entered the dressing room.

"Come on, guys, I know the Timberwolves have a couple of wins, but it ain't over yet," he admonished his forlorn teammates.

"That's not it," said defenceman Eldon Mckay.

"What is it then?"

"You haven't heard. Belanger was found dead in his car in the parking lot this morning. They figure he committed suicide. The funny thing is he was wearing an old goalie's mask."

"My God, Brunsell," whispered Chamberlin, slumping to the bench in front of his lockers.

"What?"

"Oh, nothing. It's just too bad for the guy."

Maybe Belanger had been telling the truth, thought Chamberlin. He had so easily listened to Brunsell. Who could refuse having their dreams suddenly become reality?

Even with the death, practice went ahead. Belanger had been a player. He would understand the need to prepare for the Timberwolves. Chamberlin seemed inspired. Perhaps he simply concentrated on the puck rather than the fear he felt. He stopped everything that was shot his way, even taking one off the old mask.

"Chamberlin."

"Yeah, Coach?"

"You play tonight. Maybe you can turn things around."

The butterflies were back that night as he readied himself for the game. He grabbed his old helmet. He looked at the bent cage and the worn logo. As he lifted it to his head, his eyes caught a glimpse of the painted mask. If the Cougars lost tonight, the season was over. The team was looking to him to be the difference, it was finally his moment. The painted mask seemed to beckon, but what of Brunsell? What about Belanger? Had he committed suicide or was it more of Brunsell's handiwork?

The only certainty was the importance of the game and his dream. He had to win.

Chamberlin began climbing the stairs to the ice. On the top step, he paused and looked into the stands. Usually it was just a mass of faces, each indistinguishable from the next, but tonight he could see Michelle Brunsell sitting there in the stands behind the Cougar bench.

Chamberlin stepped onto the ice and skated toward the net. The cougar, the ram and Michelle skated with him.

# Canadian Angels
*Lorna Crozier*

(written for our women's hockey team at the Olympics for the final against the Americans, February 21, 2002)

Angels of the House, Angels of Mercy—yes, they've called women that. But these are Angels of Ice. Hard-muscled, sharp, dangerous as winter's cold. How else you explain their speed, the light streaming from their helmets, the slivers of water under their burning blades that cut across the blue lines like scissors slicing through the cotton for a quilt?

Lace to these gals is lacing up. Cinnamon and allspice is slapshot, snap shot, backhand, wrist—that's the recipe they're passing on from mothers to daughters, to women like me whose brothers in our races at outdoor rinks skated backwards and beat us every time.

Break away, break away, swift angels carrying the puck, invisible wings beating, your goalie a blaze of glory in the crease.

All across the North we'll roar and cheer. You'll fly us far above the boards, above the rooftops of the rink tonight, fly us into the skate-blade brightness of the winter stars.

# Saskatchewan's Own Golden Girls
*Calvin Daniels*

It was a benchmark in women's hockey and a golden moment for Canada, and four Saskatchewan-born players were part of it.

In 2002, Canada won the Olympic gold medal in women's hockey in Salt Lake City. Hayley Wickenheiser, Dana Antal, Kelly Béchard and Colleen Sostorics stood on the blue line listening to the strains of their national anthem. The victory was huge for the sport in Canada and for the players on the ice.

Sostorics said she certainly didn't grasp the importance it had taken back in her home country.

"Call me naive, but I didn't really realize it would be as big a deal as it turned out," she said. "I knew my parents would be watching but not seven million other Canadians." The players had to keep their emotions under some level of control. "At the time you're just playing hockey," said Sostorics.

Béchard said the team simply didn't think Canada would be so moved by their win, in spite of knowing the game's popularity. "I don't think any of us realized the impact it had on the people back in Canada. I don't think we realized that until we stepped off the plane."

Wickenheiser, one of the country's top players, always looked to the Oympics as the zenith of her sport. "For me it was always the premier event in women's hockey." Antal was actually cut prior to the 1998 Olympics, so "being told I was going to the Olympics (in '02) was obviously a dream come true."

Béchard said the Olympics became a focal point for her development as a hockey player. A member of Team Saskatchewan at the Canada Games, she was scouted at age 17 to attend a national team training camp. Not only would she make the Canada under-22 team, but she had come to appreciate that hockey could lead her to the Olympics. She said having that goal helped her become a better player.

"Hockey had always been a game that I loved, something I was very passionate about," she said. "I wanted to be the best player I could be ... Going to that camp really opened my eyes to what I needed to do to achieve that."

For many on the team, the 2002 gold medal was just a bit sweeter because it followed the disappointment of losing the gold-medal game in Nagano, Japan, in 1998. "That was obviously bitter. It was tough, but it set us up well for 2002," said Wickenheiser. "We were hungry. We didn't want to experience that feeling from Nagano again. It was such a sick feeling standing on the blue line. In 2002, we had so many veterans who didn't want to feel the way they did in '98."

In Nagano, Canada went into the gold-medal game as the favorite, but was considered the underdog four years later, having lost eight meetings in a row to the American team leading up to their big game. "We had lost eight of eight to the Americans leading up to Salt Lake, but we all felt we could win that one game when it mattered the most," said Wickenheiser.

Antal said she certainly felt the veterans' desire to win in Salt Lake. "All we had on our minds was winning a gold medal. There was a feeling they (the veterans) had made some mistakes in Nagano, and maybe some regrets ... I just kind of knew this time around, leaving the gold-medal game, win or lose, they would know they had played the best they could."

Still, the gold-medal game in 2002 was a nail-biter. The Canadians led 1-0 early on a goal by Caroline Ouellette, marking the first time the Americans had trailed in the tournament. Wickenheiser would make it 2-0 early in the second, before the Americans got their first. Then with time almost expired in the second, Jayna Hefford scored what would eventually be Canada's game-winner, as they held on to win the game 3-2.

"I never thought it was ours until there were zero seconds on the clock," said Wickenheiser, adding that the feeling of the win was "unbelievable."

It was clearly an emotional time for the team and the country they represented. "The pride was seeping out of my eyeballs," said Sostorics. "It was my happy place, too—the flag being raised, the national anthem being played and the gold medal around your neck."

The feeling almost escaped description for Béchard, who added that the emotion hit home as the final buzzer sounded. "It was the most pride you could ever feel hearing the national anthem played," she said. "You look down and your teammates are getting their gold medals, and then it's put around your neck—it's something I dreamed about my whole athletic career. It's unbelievable."

Although they went into the game as underdogs, Béchard said there was a surprising relaxed calm around the team. "I think as a team we were all really prepared for the game. We knew as a team we had done everything we could to prepare for that game. We knew player for player we were definitely more talented. It was just a matter of putting everything together and playing an outstanding game."

Antal said there was no doubt in her mind the team would be in the gold-medal game. She added that, while it might seem arrogant, she expected to win. "I never thought we were going to lose that game after it started," she said. "There was a feeling when that puck dropped, we were going to win that game. And when it was over, there was almost relief. We were just unbelievably happy to have worked that hard and won. When you've worked so hard, it's so much more worthwhile in the end."

Going into the game, Sostorics said, it was a case of trying to maintain the regime as it had been before any other game, playing hacky sack and trying to stay loose. "I don't remember being particularly nervous. We were just going through the same routine," she said. Once the game started, penalties piled up for the Canadians and, Sostorics said, "It was a case of hitting the bench, catching our breath and going back to kill another penalty." Killing the string of penalties actually allowed Sostorics a feeling the team was doing all right in the game. "It was kind of surreal how everybody presented themselves in different situations."

Each of the Golden Girls had similar starts in hockey. For Wickenheiser, it was almost in her genes. "Dad (Tom) played old-timers hockey and we used to go to the rink quite a bit," she said. "I can remember being pulled on my sled to the rink and asking my mom (Marilyn) if I could play hockey." The first step was a family backyard rink for her and her siblings. From there it was a natural to start playing organized hockey in her hometown of Shaunavon. Of course, that meant playing with the boys. "I didn't see it as a big deal, having a girl playing hockey," she said, adding that in a small town, "I was just another body to help make the team work."

For Antal, hockey was her parents' suggestion. "My parents just asked me if I wanted to play hockey," she said, adding that it was somewhat unique. "Back then there weren't a lot of parents asking their daughters if they wanted to play hockey." In Esterhazy, Saskatchewan, that meant joining the boys on the ice, too. "I was really, really fortunate. The boys I played hockey with in Esterhazy were all kids I went to school with, so it didn't seem to matter whether I was a boy or a girl."

At four, Sostorics began to skate and play the game, but she doesn't have a personal recollection of why. "The story goes that I just asked if I could play. My parents put me in some of my older brother's old equipment and away I went." It was an immediate match, hockey and Sostorics. "I love everything about it. I love the ice, the fast pace, the physical play. It just feels right for me."

She would play on the local boys' team in Kennedy until she completed high school. The small town allowed her lots of ice time and playing with the boys forced her development because of their size and strength. "I could have been on the ice every day."

Béchard's older sister had started to play hockey on a team coached by an uncle, and Kelly quickly followed her lead. "I started playing when I was five. Growing up in a small town (Sedley, population 350), there's not a lot of kids to play," she said, adding that her sister was the draw. "Growing up, you always idolize your older siblings." Béchard was 14 when she joined her first all-female team, a bantam girls' team in Regina that played against peewee boys. "I remember it was very competitive."

As Wickenheiser grew older, she said there was the issue of dressing room space as she continued on boys' teams, and in some cases there were a few people jealous of the ice time a girl was taking away from the boys. "But my parents were great, they always sheltered me from that stuff. I think Mom and Dad heard some of that stuff, but they didn't worry me about it."

As Antal got older, hockey lost its lustre for a time. In her first year of contact hockey, she found it wasn't something she relished. "I really didn't enjoy it at all. I didn't really like being the only girl on a boys' team," she said. Antal would play a little girls' hockey, travelling hours for games, but she said her ice time was sporadic. "Once I started playing hockey with the girls, I didn't play a lot of organized games." Then, as she completed high school, Cornell University came calling. "At the time there weren't a lot of Canadian girls heading down to the U.S. colleges," but she took the plunge, spending two seasons there. "It was not really a means to an end. It was just an opportunity which I decided to take."

Antal came back to Canada after being selected for the women's national program. "I was far from ready to be playing at the international level," she said. "I was released from that team after a couple months." While admitting that it was hard to accept she wasn't good enough, it set her on a mission. "I realized trying to make the national team was something I had to go for." So she moved back to Calgary to play with the best players. "They were doing things quicker and faster and stronger. I was put in a position I had to do things at a higher level just to survive on a day-to-day basis." The work paid off when she made the 2002 team.

Sostorics also made a move after high school, heading to Calgary to play with the University of Calgary Dinosaurs and a senior women's team. Both were preludes to making the Canadian under-22 national team in 1998. She would play on the team for three years. She admitted the step up to the national stage was a big one. "I think every level you move up is a substantial jump.

Everything is a little bit faster. You have to think a little bit faster," she said. Playing on the under-22 team was a great experience because it helped her prepare for the next step to the national team. "It gets the nerves of wearing the Maple Leaf on your sweater well over," she said. Pulling on the sweater for the first time certainly carries emotions with it. "It's something you've dreamed about and when you finally do it, it's an amazing feeling." In 2001, Sostorics made the national team, and it, too, was a big step. "We always say you're playing with the big girls now." Sostoric's selection was never totally expected, as she was one of 30 who started out. "You had to prove yourself that whole year. I was just working hard every day. I'm not sure it even crossed my mind that I'd be in the Olympics."

Béchard also headed to Calgary after high school with the goal of becoming a better hockey player and getting her education. She said the under-22 team was a sort of bridge to finally making the national team, where she won gold medals at the world championships in both 2000 and 2001, events she said emotionally rivaled the Olympic victory for her.

Wickenheiser's skill level made her one of the better players on most teams she played on. Such skills also allowed her to dream a hockey dream that she shared with almost every Canadian boy. "I always dreamed I would play in the NHL one day. I'd play with either the Oilers or the Canadiens," she said. However, by the time she was 11 or 12, she realized "it was going to be a lot more difficult being a female player in hockey." So her NHL dream faded. Then, in 1990, the first women's world hockey championship was held. "I watched the 1990 world championships in Calgary. I was very inspired by that," said Wickenheiser.

A couple of years later, she was in British Columbia at a hockey school when more good news came. "Mom came running in and said women's hockey had been accepted as a gold-medal sport in the Olympics. I remember thinking from that point on, I had a purpose."

For Wickenheiser, that purpose will continue as she plans to play in the 2006 Olympics and has an eye set on 2010 in Vancouver as well. Antal also wants to be back in 2006. "That's my goal right now, because it was such a positive experience in 2002," she said.

Sostorics wants to go back, too, having nothing but good memories of Salt Lake City. Both on the ice and off. She said simply being part of the opening ceremonies was beyond words. "It was sort of a feeling that is very hard to explain." She remembers walking into the stadium and just to the left seeing a gathering of screaming, flag-waving Canadian supporters. "I don't know if I shed a tear, but I know I felt like it." Béchard wants the feeling of the Olympics at least once more. "I want to win another one and I want to be a more important part of that win. I think I still have a few years left to give to the team and to the program."

Having four members of the gold-winning team from Saskatchewan doesn't surprise Wickenheiser. "I think Saskatchewan tends to produce hard-working, good character players."

## Art Is International and Has No Borders
### *Don Kerr*

You want me to cheer for just hockey?
Hockey its own self? Well, you know
I'm no Platonist, eh, I'm from Saskatoon
and I cheer for the Saskatoon Blades.
You remember Federko? Behind the net
with a stick that had glue on it?
Chapman and his brother Chapman,
Hajt, Williams, Kortko, Zakreskie,
Price, Hamilton, Pinder, and his brother
Pinder, Hawryliw, Klassen.
That's who. Playing in the Arena
built by public subscription
in the depth of the Depression.
Me and my dad went since 1947
and sat top row west end,
see the enemy goal
two periods out of three.

But I am not just a parochial
local fan eh. I got wider horizons.
I live and die with the Montreal Canadiens
and even defend French TV because they
bring my games. Premiere etoile.
You see Aurel Joliat take his last slow
skate around the Forum?
Saskatoon Sheiks traded him to the
Canadiens in 1923. Did you know that?

My dad came from Nokomis like Elmer Lach
who centred Richard and Blake,
the Punch Line. Lucky my dad didn't come from
Wilcox where the Metz brothers came from
or I'd have to cheer for the Leafs.

## Bienfait, Saskatchewan
December 1997
*Bill Boyd*

Frank Pastachak is six foot three and weighs 275 pounds. He has hands the size of hams and the face of a defensive tackle from the days before face masks. But his game isn't football, it's hockey. "I can hardly wait until fall comes and the ice goes in and it starts again for another year," he says. His voice is a cross between a bark and a growl. "It's the travelling, it's the crowds, it's the people in hockey, it's everything. It's even better when you have your boys playing. I love hockey's intensity. And you've got to be tough to play, but you've got to have finesse. It demands everything. You got to be able to take your bumps and bruises. There's not a game can touch it. Not even goddamn close."

Frank Pastachak's team is the Bienfait Coalers. Bienfait—pronounced *been-fate*—is in coal-mining country a few miles east of Estevan, tucked into that tidy corner of the map where Saskatchewan, Manitoba and North Dakota meet at right angles. There's not much to it, although its story has its colourful, and tragic, chapters. In 1920 there was a gangland slaying, never solved, which apparently was connected to the booze that was trucked through Bienfait and into the United States during Prohibition. And in the cemetery are the bodies of three coal miners. The miners died during a strike in 1931. A headstone says simply: "Murdered by the RCMP."

Pastachak is retired. For years he was the town of Bienfait's chief maintenance man. As a young man he played some senior hockey and then he got into officiating. "The referees were always neutral but the teams would supply a linesman each and pay him 10 dollars a game," he says. "That's what I did. I'd leave work at 5 o'clock, get on the old school bus we'd fixed up for the team — sometimes I'd drive it — and we'd be off 80, 90 miles to play. I'd officiate, drive back, maybe 2 or 3 in the morning, some nights snowing so bad you could see better with the headlights off, and go to work at 7 o'clock.

I'm not an on-ice official anymore, but I do some goal-judging and I try to line up prizes from local merchants like gift coupons and stuff for the draws between periods. Anything to make money for the team. And I'll still travel when the team does. I get excited as hell at games. I got in a fight last year with a ref, because he wasn't calling anything. Some of our guys could have been damn near killed, but no penalties. But the cops couldn't do anything to me. They didn't see nothing. It was my word against the ref's."

Tonight, a Sunday night, Pastachak is getting excited. It's the Coalers' first game of the season. They are playing the Carnduff Red Devils in Bienfait. The rink is just across the street from the Pastachak house. "Not bad, eh?" he says. "Some nights I don't even bother with a coat." The Coalers are in a senior league like Stonewall's. It's called the Big Six, which is something like the Group of Seven. That's to say, the number doesn't mean much. This year the Big Six has eight teams; one year it had five, and it's had as many as 12. It's been around a long time. "It's a tough league, believe me," Pastachak says. He leaves his house for the 30-second walk to the rink. It's mild for early December so he's wearing only a light jacket. "Jesus, I hope we get some people tonight," he says.

Pastachak estimates the Coalers' budget at $10,000, most of it going to travel and sticks. Echoing Stonewall's complaint, he says that some teams pay their players as much as $300 or $400 each game. "That's horseshit for a league like this," he says. "We can't afford it. We give them sticks and tape, that's it. We don't draw that good, maybe a hundred or so."

Both of Frank Pastachak's sons — Kevin, who is 32, and Kelly, 25 — play for the Coalers. Kevin was asked to join another team for pay but stayed at home. He has two children and he works for the Prairie Coal Corp. as an oiler-operator on a dragline, the huge mechanical bucket used in surface mining. He's tall, like his father, but slim and much more relaxed.

"I was always at the rink when I was a kid, tagging along after my dad when he was officiating," Kevin says. "I'd have my skates and some of the players would come out on the ice and show me a few things. And when I was around 14, four of us would go to the rink at 1 in the morning on weekends and play two-on-two. And we'd clean the ice between periods at Coaler games before they got a Zamboni. We'd wear skates and push scrapers. Growing up, a bunch of us always competed with each other, and that's bound to make you a better player. In the summer, when the ice was out, we set up nets and we played with a ball."

Frank Pastachak says, "One year, when Kevin was playing juvenile in Lampman, right after the game he and three others jumped in the car, didn't even take off their skates, drove 20 miles to Bienfait, changed sweaters and went out to play for the Coalers. They got there for the second period and we're losing 4-1. We won in the end and it was because of Kevin and the three others."

Kevin also played for the Estevan Bruins in the Saskatchewan junior league. One of his coaches was Gerry James, the great running back with the Winnipeg Blue Bombers in the '50s who'd played a bit for the Toronto Maple Leafs.

"He knew how to get the best out of us," Kevin says. "He knew that everyone is different and had to be treated differently." He says that James was one of the first coaches he'd heard of who used aerobics. "I think we were doing them long before other teams.

"But I could get mad at him. One night we're in North Battleford and I'm on the number 1 line. We scored on a power play but that wasn't good enough because we hadn't done the power play his way. So he sat us out for the whole period. I was on 99 points for the season. I really wanted a hundred, but I didn't get it. I didn't say anything, though, and neither did he."

As Frank Pastachak enters the rink, a number of people greet him. A woman asks for his wife. "She's coming in a few minutes," he tells her. At the snack bar, the coffee comes in china mugs. "How many rinks have you been to where they serve it like this?" asks a young woman. "People donate them. Better than Styrofoam or paper cups, eh?"

Frank says that the Coaler players' jobs make it difficult for them all to get out to practice at the same time. "They're working shifts in the oilfields, for the mines," he says. "They don't get any breaks from their employers." He says that teams are allowed rosters of 20 or 21 but that only 16 have signed with the Coalers and they can only count on 10 or 12 on any given night.

James Wrigley, a squat man in a wool coat, likes hockey as much as Frank Pastachak does. For a living, he drives a truck for the Estevan Coal Corporation. When he lived in Calgary, he says, he'd occasionally drive the bus for the New Westminster Bruins — who used to be the Estevan Bruins — when they were on their Prairie swings. "Just being around hockey players is good," he says. James' son Jamie, a defenceman built like Tie Domi, is the Coalers captain. Right after the game he has to report for his night shift as a dragline operator with Prairie Coal. James Wrigley worries that there aren't enough players coming up with his son's kind of dedication to what he calls "good old hockey." He says, "That's sad because small-town hockey used to be the best thing going on. It's what kept towns together, gave them their identity."

The Bienfait rink is an old rink with dressing rooms upstairs. The players must walk down to the ice through knots of spectators. But the ice is good and there's more of it than in many rinks. Kevin Pastachak played seven years in Germany. He likes the European-sized surfaces. He says the Bienfait rink is 87 feet wide. That's two feet wider than the standard NHL rink. Kevin dropped back from forward to defence a couple of years ago. Like Jamie Wrigley, he's able to control the pace of the game.

"When we went to see Kevin in Germany, they treated us like royalty," Frank Pastachak says. "There'd be six or seven thousand at a game and Kevin would be picked as most valuable player and they'd all stand and cheer him. You're so goddamn proud. There's nothing like it."

Craig Kickley, who says he's lucky to be walking, is a slight, fair man of 33. He's been playing in the Big Six since he was 16. This would be his seventh season with the Coalers, but he's out with a serious neck injury. He was checked into the boards from behind in an exhibition game. He says, "The doctor told me a fraction closer to the spinal cord and I'd be in a wheelchair now and—"

Frank Pastachak interrupts. "They didn't even call a goddamn penalty," he barks. "The guy should have been kicked out of the league. The officiating is goddamn awful sometimes. They don't know what the hell they're doing."

Kickley says that people have advised him to quit. "But I hate just watching. I want to play. Hell, people have come back from neck injuries." Until he can play again, he's putting together a book on the league's history. "When you're a kid, you'd look up to senior players with stars in your eyes," he says. "It may sound crazy, but they were like gods. People from the cities don't understand how important hockey is to places like Bienfait."

Kickley, Frank Pastachak and James Wrigley are standing with a handful of other men on the balcony at the end of the rink, outside the dressing rooms. Nothing is between them and the Carnduff goal about 15 feet below. "You got to be goddamn quick to duck if the puck gets deflected up here," Frank says.

Duane Kocoy, who's doing play-by-play for CJSL Radio in Estevan, is up there, too, mic in hand, with no protection. His equipment is on a chair in front of him. Downstairs, behind the glass, there's maybe 70 people. A few more are scattered in the two rows of unheated seats along the boards. Frank Pastachak gives the house the once-over, like a veteran vaudevillian. "Crowds'll pick up after Christmas," he says, almost with certainty.

In the first period Bienfait has three power plays. During a two-man advantage, Kevin moves in from the point and lets go a hard, rising shot. The puck is deflected. It hits the goalie's arm and bounces well over his head. He loses sight of it. He still hasn't found it when it drops down behind him, trickles off the crossbar and falls harmlessly into the mesh at the back of the net. "Jesus Christ, can you believe that," Frank Pastachak says.

A moment later a Coaler breaks in alone across the Carnduff blue line. A linesman stops the play: a two-line pass. The crowd boos. At rinkside, a skinny young man with a beard and wearing a grubby Philadelphia Flyers windbreaker leans toward the linesman, who's against the boards, about three feet from him. "I hate to say it," the skinny man shouts over the booing, almost into the linesman's ear, "but that was a good call." The linesman looks up, winks and then skates away, following the play. "I don't give a shit if it was against Bienfait," the skinny man says to his companion. "It was a good call. He took the pass over the line."

Gradually, the Red Devils take control. In the second period they score three goals, two within a couple of minutes. "I think this is their fourth game,"

Pastachak says. "Not like us." He's not a good loser. With the score 5-0 in the third, Pastachak and some others begin to taunt the Red Devil goalie, just below them. Play is stopped. The goalie says something to the referee. "What the hell you crying about?" Pastachak yells at him. The goalie has told the ref that they're spitting on him. "Christ, we're not goddamn well spitting on him," Pastachak tells the RCMP constable who has come up to check things out. He is a youngster, in glasses, about half Frank's size. "Yeah, no one's been spitting on him," James Wrigley agrees. Frank Pastachak says loudly, as much to the goalie as to the RCMP constable. "For Christ's sake, can't the little baby take some yelling?" Another man says, "Yeah, poor baby can't take it." The goalie never turns around. The young cop sighs audibly and raises his eyebrows in mock resignation. "Just take it easy then," he says. "Let's have no spitting." He moves off down the stairs. Duane Kocoy, the broadcaster, has been doubled over his equipment, trying to protect it from the people pushing around him. The game ends and in spite of the chippiness, the players shake hands. Kelly Pastachak, Frank's second son, goes over to the boards and picks up his infant daughter, Jessica Blair, and takes her for a little skate, holding her up to be seen, and the crowd cheers. Frank watches his son and granddaughter. "That's nice," he says.

The crush of bodies begins to thin and Kocoy sets about packing up his equipment. He says that he learned broadcasting at school in Regina and moved down to Estevan's CJSL about 10 years ago. He says that Bienfait is the hardest rink to work from. "The other rinks, some have areas designed for me," he says. "But to be fair, even here, the guys standing close are just listening to me call the game. They seldom give me any trouble." Then, trying to choose his words carefully, he says that Frank Pastachak and James Wrigley can be difficult in the heat of a game. "That shouldn't surprise you, though," he says. "You've seen them. But they're sure as hell the most dedicated fans. You can't fault them there. There's no one like them. I guess that's what hockey needs in places like this."

Kocoy used to broadcast the Estevan Bruins games. He gave them up because he didn't like the travel. He's 30 years old, married, and has two young sons. "With the senior hockey it's an hour and a half on a bus at most," he says. "That's a far cry from five hours to Yorkton with the Bruins or a weekend northern trip. And I realized that if I can't hack the junior A travel, I sure as hell couldn't handle anything higher than that. So for now at least, I'm very happy here. I love calling games.

"We're a little down on the dial so we don't have the greatest reach, so we might get maybe two hours north. And it's not a huge money-maker, but it's important. They can listen to their kids and grandkids play senior hockey. That means a lot to the parents in Oxbow or Redvers. I hear about shut-ins in Carlyle who like nothing better than to listen to the Carlyle Cougars on the radio. For me it's a bit like being a big fish in a little pond, but it's still nice.

"And remember, for some of these guys, this is their NHL. For some of them, to have their games broadcast on the radio is a big deal. Sometimes they'll tape the games, play them back, and if they don't like something I've said, they'll let me know.

"I think the hardest thing I ever did was a quadruple-overtime game by myself. It was a playoff between Bienfait and Carlyle two years ago. It was here and the rink was packed. God, they were stacked in, breaking every fire law in the land. I couldn't move for five hours. I was on the air from 8 o'clock to after 1. All by myself, even the between-period intermissions."

Frank Pastachak has said his goodnights and is on his way across the street to his home. "Ah hell," he says. "That's just first-game jitters. A few more practices and a few more games and we'll be fine." He's calmed down. It's hard to believe he was so worked up only a few minutes ago. "I can't explain it," he says. "Hockey does that to me. It always has." It's getting colder. Most of the fans have gone. For a moment, it's very still and quiet. There's no moon, but beyond the arena, under the pale light from the stars, the prairie stretches to the horizon. And out on it, perhaps miles away, a train really does whistle and a dog really does howl.

## Johnny
### Stephen Scriver

Even in my boozed-up glow
the old drunk offends me
barging into our table
in Rouleau pub coughing
and picking up a draught

he looks away from my scowl
to my jacket
*Grenfell Hockey Club eh?*
*Y'know I played for P.A. Mintos '34 to '36*

I smirk into my glass
then look at my buddy
Sure    *Old hockey players don't die*
*They just lose their cans*
but he's not laughing

the old guy coughs and goes on
*Yep had a shot at the Leafs in '37*
I cough a mouthful
and look at my buddy who sez
*Show him the clippings Johnny*

and he lifts a pouch
from his Sally Ann coat
and pushes it at me

and I read
"Gervais Scores Four in Playoff Romp ....
speedy little centreman ...
sensational stickhandling display ...
scouts from the NHL ..."

and I look from words to man
and back to words
till my hesitant eyes get him going

primed on free beer
he's really into it
how the stick in his hands charmed the puck
how the goalies he deked could fill a stadium
and how the booze and bad lungs got to him
before he laced on those big-time skates

and I can only listen and pay
wonder if some day I'll need free beer

## Max Bentley and the Hockey Pants
### Robert Currie

"With Max Bentley?" I said. "You?" I was halfway out the door, my hockey stick slung over my shoulder, when I overheard my parents talking and wheeled back into the kitchen. The grin on my father's face made his teeth shine like the Stanley Cup. For two years in a row, Max Bentley had led the NHL in scoring, with 72 points this year, and in 1946 with 61 points in only 47 games. He was the best stickhandler in the world.

"Sure," Pop said. "I thought you knew that."

"I knew you used to know him."

"Course, I did play more with his older brothers, Roy and Scoop. They were closer to my age. In Delisle everybody played—"

"But you played with Max Bentley? Really?"

"Yes, Jamie, I played with Max. He was just a kid at the time and I was getting on, almost too old for the senior team, but, yes, we played a few games together."

"Did you ever go against him — in practice, I mean?"

My father grinned even wider. "You know those hockey pants down in the cellar?" he asked.

Hanging on a nail behind the cellar stairs was an old-fashioned pair of hockey pants, the material a worn and faded canvas, the protection provided by thin wooden slats sewn beneath the outer fabric. On the right leg, two of the slats were broken.

"Those things?" I said. "They're so old, they're falling apart."

"They're old," he said, "but that's not why they're falling apart. The last time I wore them was the last scrimmage I ever played against Max Bentley."

"You never told me any of this," said Mom.

"What happened, Pop?"

There was a thump on the floor beside me. I looked down. Lying on the kitchen linoleum was my hockey stick. I'd forgotten I was holding it.

"Take it easy," Pop said. "You don't want to scratch your mother's new floor."

I stooped and grabbed the stick. "Come on, Pop. Tell me what happened."

"Well, Max was just a kid, maybe a couple years older than you, but his brothers could already see he'd be NHL material someday. So they had him out with the Delisle Seniors. They'd let him play a couple shifts every game—that was all. I mean, some of us were 10, 20 years older than him. In practice, though, we were always short of players. They used to let him centre a line with two of his older brothers. I'll tell you something—you could see that kid improve every day."

"Yeah, Pop, but what about the pants?"

"You know what the papers say about his wrist shot?"

"Sure," I said, "It's his strong wrists. He milks all those—"

"Uh-huh. You've been reading the sports pages. Well, maybe he does milk the odd cow," said Pop, rubbing his mouth with his knuckles. "He's got a whale of a wrist shot, that's for sure."

"He's the dipsy-doodle-dandy from Delisle!"

"Enough, Jamie," said Mom.

"Anyway, in practice one day, he and Roy come swooping down the ice." Pop grabbed my stick, flicked it from side to side. "Roy feeds him a pass at the blue line. I'm on defence, kind of cruising backwards, just waiting for him to make a move. But before I know what's happening, he's flicked those wrists and the puck is flying straight at me. Caught it right here." He slapped his upper thigh. "Broke the slats in my pants, left a bruise dark as a coal chute. I must've limped for a week."

I was staring at him, had been staring, I guess, ever since he'd begun to describe Max Bentley swooping toward him.

"Close the flytrap," Mom said. I closed my mouth, teeth snapping together.

"Is it still there?" I asked.

"What?"

"The bruise on your leg."

"Don't be silly," he said. He reached out, tousled my hair, then gave me a little push toward the door. "You better get going. It's bedtime in an hour."

"Uh-huh." Already he'd disappeared behind the front page of the *Times Herald*.

"Those pants downstairs. Do you think maybe I could wear them tonight?"

At first he didn't move or speak. Then, when he lowered the newspaper, I could see he was grinning from the comic strips. "Well," he said, "I sure won't be wearing them anymore. You go right ahead — just as long as you can find a way to keep them from falling down around your ankles."

They were kind of big.

When I hauled them down from the nail under the steps, I shook enough dust off them to clog the drain. I could feel the broken slats in the leg. Right there was where Max Bentley's shot had hit. I pulled them over my breeches, but they were eight or 10 inches too big at the waist. Scrambling around on Pop's workbench, I found some twine that I cut into two pieces and tied onto the pants like suspenders. Maybe with my Black Hawk sweater on, nobody would notice how badly the pants fitted.

It was kind of awkward going up the stairs because the pants hung down so far I could hardly bend my knees. I made it okay, though, grabbed my stick and trotted down to the corner of Elsom Street where the guys were all under the street light, playing road hockey with an India rubber ball. We had months and months to wait before there'd be ice on the outdoor rinks again.

"Whose side am I on?" I asked. "I'm gonna be Max Bentley."

"I'm already Max Bentley," said my friend Tim, who lived right next to the Skipton Road rink. "You can be Ted Lindsay if you want. Nobody's got him yet."

"Naw, he plays dirty. I wanna be Max Bentley."

"Max Bentley's taken," said one of the bigger kids. It was Ray, one of the twins. He was always Wild Bill Ezinicki because he liked to fight—especially with his brother. "Be Syl Apps, be Leo Reise. What difference does it make?"

"Lots," I said. "You see these hockey pants?"

"Is that what they are?" said his brother Reg. "I thought you had a horse blanket wrapped around your butt."

"Come on!" I said. "See these broken slats? My pop was wearing these pants when it happened. That's where Max Bentley hit him with a wrist shot. Whap! And he couldn't walk for a month."

"Aw, your father's moustache," said Ray. "Listen. You're Leo Reise and you're on their side. Now let's go."

I was sure glad none of the girls were around to watch. When Pop called me in, we were losing 17-15, and I'd only scored one goal. That's because Leo Reise was a defenceman and he hardly ever got a goal. Last year he played 48 games for Chicago and Detroit and he only had four goals. If they'd let me be Max Bentley, I'd have scored at least a hat trick. I know I would have.

★★★

Next morning when I sat down at the breakfast table, I found out why Mom and Pop had been talking about Max Bentley.

"We didn't want to tell you last night," said Pop. "You wouldn't have slept a wink."

I was scooping brown sugar onto my Cream of Wheat, trying to snitch an extra spoonful before Mom slapped the lid back on the sugar jar.

"Oh, go ahead. Dig in," Mom said, grinning. "He's coming tonight for supper."

"Who is?" I heaped another spoon of sugar on my porridge.

"Who are we talking about?" asked Pop. "Max Bentley, that's who."

"Max Bentley!" I knew I'd scattered sugar on the table, but I didn't care. "Here? He's coming here? For supper?"

"Yes, here," said Mom. "This is where we have our supper, isn't it?"

"You're not just kidding me?"

"Of course not," said Pop.

"Yeah, but — why would he be coming here?"

"He's on some kind of tour before he heads home. As you well know, the Hawks got knocked out early. He's hitting a lot of different cities."

"Yeah but — our house?"

"Listen, 'yeah but'," said Pop, "you can believe me." He stared at me a minute and shrugged before continuing. "Our families were close back in Delisle. We know each other. He's coming for a visit."

"And a home-cooked meal," said Mom. "He's probably tired of eating those sick-looking canned peas they hand out in cafes."

It was true, then. Max Bentley was coming for supper.

"Can I have the guys over to meet him?"

Before I'd even finished asking, Pop was shaking his head. "No, son, what he'll need is a break."

"I can get his autograph, can't I? We can talk hockey."

"Sure, son." He reached across the table to rumple my hair. "You can talk hockey just as long as he wants to. But don't pester him."

"I won't." I pushed my chair back from the table.

"Where are you going?"

"Across the street. I'm gonna tell the guys—"

"Finish your porridge," Mom said. "You can tell the guys at school."

Well, I told them, all right, and they were nearly as excited as I was. In fact, that night, the twins and at least half a dozen other guys were hanging around outside, crouching against our fence, poking each other and wrestling around, just waiting to catch a glimpse of Max Bentley. I was leaning on the back of the chesterfield, my nose pressed against the picture window so I'd see his cab the second it turned the corner.

"Jamie," my father called from the next room. He was in the kitchen, mashing potatoes for my mother. "You better get ready for supper."

"I washed already."

"Well, change then. You can't eat like that."

I'd hoped he wouldn't notice. I looked down at my hockey pants, knowing full well that I couldn't tell my father I was planning to wear them to the supper table. How else could I be sure that Max Bentley would know that I was a hockey player too?

"In a minute, Pop. I can't leave right now or I might miss him."

When I turned back to the window, I saw a Grant Hall taxi round the corner. The kids weren't horsing around now; they were all staring at the taxi, almost standing at attention, except for Reg, who grabbed the door handle and jumped onto the running board, staring into the window as the car pulled into the curb. The driver must have yelled at him then because he jumped off and turned away. When the taxi door opened, they all seemed to lose interest and went back to swinging on the fence. It was just some little guy with a big nose. Heck, he wasn't much taller than Reg and Ray — and they were just in Grade 6.

Whoever this guy was, he was coming up our sidewalk. I hurried to the door, hoping he wasn't going to hang around and spoil things. He couldn't be coming for supper too. I didn't want some stranger butting in when Max Bentley was telling me how to cut across the crease and pull the goalie so I could backhand the puck into the upper corner of the net. Before the stranger had a chance to knock, I opened the door a crack.

"Yes?"

"Oh! Hi," he said. "I didn't see you standing there." He looked down at my pants, a puzzled expression flitting across his face. "Is your father in?"

"Sure." I couldn't just leave him standing in the doorway. "Come on in. Pop!" I hollered over my shoulder. "It's for you."

My father stepped out of the kitchen. "Ah," he said, "it's good to see you, Max."

"Max?" I whirled around. "You're Max Bentley?"

"That's right."

But he didn't look like a hockey player. He wasn't even as big as my father and he wasn't nearly as tough-looking as Mrs. Dunlop, my Grade 5 teacher.

"This is my son Jamie," Pop said. He slapped me on the rear. "You can see he's a hockey player too."

"I noticed the pants," said Max Bentley. He winked at my dad. "They look like something King Clancy wore back in the '20s. So — how's Jean doing?"

"Fine. She's in the kitchen, just about ready to pull a chicken out of the oven."

"Now you're talking my language," said Max Bentley, and he strode into the kitchen to see my mother. "Oooh Jeannie. Those Chicago girls look like mops alongside you." When Pop turned to follow him, I gave a yank at his sleeve.

"Isn't he going to talk hockey?"

"Later on, I'm sure he will. Now don't be a bother."

"Can I get his autograph? I can do that now, can't I?"

"Sure," Pop grinned down at me. "He's used to autographs. Go ahead."

As I ran to my bookshelf for my autograph book, I could already picture what he'd write: "Max Bentley, NHL all-star, Leading scorer, 1945/47." Then, if he stopped and thought about it, maybe he'd scrawl another line across the bottom of the page: "See you in the NHL someday."

My autograph book was really neat. It had a cover made of real leather, and every page was a different colour. I planned to use it exclusively for important people, although so far there was only one autograph in the book and that had come from my cousin Brian, who'd signed the book before he'd given it to me for Christmas.

I knew my face was flushed when I carried the autograph book into the kitchen. Mom had the chicken out of the oven and sitting on top of the stove, but she was just talking to Max Bentley, hadn't even started to scoop out the dressing. "You always were the charmer," she said. As soon as she stopped talking, I jumped right in, autograph book poised.

"Excuse me, Max Bentley."

"Mr. Bentley!" said my mother.

"Max is fine," he said at almost the same time.

"Max," I said, "I was wondering, Max, if I could get your autograph."

"Sure." He reached for the book, took it from my hand, flipped to page 2, but didn't sign. Was he going to change his mind? "I'll need a pen," he said.

"Oh, yeah. Sure, Max." I ran for the desk in the bedroom, hurling myself through the narrow hall, the yards of fabric in my hockey pants dusting off the lower shelves of the hall bookcase, knocking three of my mother's ornaments onto the rug. The calico cat and two ceramic chickens. Nothing broken. I'd pick them up later. I yanked open the desk drawer, found my father's Waterman fountain pen, spun open the bottle of dark blue ink, filled the pen and headed for the kitchen, sideways through the hall so my hockey pants wouldn't collide with more ornaments.

"Here's the pen," I said, sliding into the kitchen.

"Well," he said, "I'd better make it a good one."

He took the pen but didn't write anything at first. Instead he looked out the kitchen window, the pen poised by his mouth. When he lowered the pen to paper, there was a faint blue smudge on his lower lip. Staring at the page from across the table and upside down too, I couldn't tell what he was writing, but he was writing lots. Maybe he was saying that he wanted me for his left-winger someday. He wrote another line. And another. Then he blew on the page, closed the book and pushed it across the table to me.

"Thanks Max," I said. "Thanks a lot." I grabbed the book and headed for my room in the basement. This was gonna be great. I didn't need anyone looking over my shoulder when I read it. Man, the guys would just croak with envy when they saw it.

Slamming the door behind me, I flung myself on my bed and opened the book. Page 2 was covered with writing. "To Jamie," it said at the top; below, Max Bentley had written: "I wish I was a little fishie/ Frozen in the ice/ And when the girls came skating by/ Wouldn't that be nice!/ Your pal, Max Bentley."

I read it again. That was what it said, all right. A bunch of wimpy, sissy stuff.

I flung the book to the floor, where it bounced once before skidding under my dresser. It could darn well stay there, too.

I rolled over, sat up on my bed. Something was poking me in the stomach. I looked down. My hockey pants were all scrunched up on my legs, one of the broken struts jabbing me in the gut. My shins stuck out from beneath the pants like they belonged to somebody sitting in a pup tent that had just collapsed on top of him. Silly—that was how the pants looked, how I looked.

I pulled the pants off, carried them out of my room. At first, I thought I'd hang them back under the cellar stairs, but instead I just threw them against the wall. When they hit, something fell, landing on the cement with a clatter, then rattling over the rough floor like a giant rolling pin.

I switched on the light.

My dad's baseball bat had cracked against the wall, bounced off it, then rolled slowly back and stopped with a click. It was a Louisville Slugger, the label dark brown on blond wood, and, burned into it, the signature of Joe DiMaggio. I ran my fingers over the name, the tip of my index finger tracing the curve of the twin g's.

I wondered if Pop ever played with the Yankee Clipper. No, probably not.

When they called me for supper, I went back upstairs. After we finished the chicken, while Mom was clearing the table, I told Max Bentley that I was a left-winger for the King Edward Hawks. "Good for you," he said, but I could see that he didn't care much. He looked tired. He wanted to talk about Pop's job at the stockyards, about what it was like every day being at work by 8 in the morning. I lost interest and wandered off when we finished dessert.

But later that night, when I was warm and drowsy in bed, just as I fell asleep, I pictured a frozen lake, the ice crystalline, clear as the night air, and all the girls in the class, skating in slow circles, long, graceful strides, white legs flashing, and there in the silver moonlight, Max Bentley floating beneath them, suspended there in a mirror of moonlight, a huge smile on his face and looking a bit like me.

# Farm Team
## *Laurie Muirhead*

The neighbour boys arrived on old throttled-down toboggans
skates on stick, hanging from a shoulder
always ready to play

We laced up on cold yellow bales
our red woollen scarves and rawhide gloves
we were Canadian … Eh!

Down the hill we trekked
through frozen dung, the nearest slough
via father's bull pen

The ice a glassy fizz, snapped and cracked
our skate blades dull, cut and scraped
rallied for position

A crowd of curious cattle gathered, a bunch of ol' boys
wrapped in burly coats, puffed cigars
cheered for the farm team

Only the boys had sticks, us girls
thrown together, used poplar branches
curved at one end

An elbow, cross-check, trip if we had to
they wouldn't dare hit a girl, didn't matter anyway
they always won!

# Aboriginal Title Comes to a Young Team
## Calvin Daniels

Team Saskatchewan won the Men's 2003 National Aboriginal Hockey Tournament. It was only the second year the Aboriginal championship for bantam- and midget-aged players was held, and the first time a male team from Saskatchewan had taken part. The tournament was played in Ontario at Akwesasne/Cornwall and was only open to teams comprised of players and coaches who were of Aboriginal ancestry.

Barry Sparvier of the Ochapowace First Nation was a member of the championship team, wearing the captain's jersey, as well as leading the team in scoring, with three goals and eight assists for 11 points in the six games played. Sparvier was also named to the male all-star team, along with three other members of the Saskatchewan team: Craig Morningchild in goal, Justin Magnuson and Travis Gardipy.

Sparvier said the Saskatchewan team was an interesting mix. While he was the only Saskatchewan Junior Hockey League player, there were others from junior B, AAA midget, and AA midget. "There were lots of personalities," he said. "We had some jokesters and we had some serious guys, but we bonded pretty quickly." As for wearing the "C," Sparvier said it was a tremendous honour. "It was great to be captain and share my experience playing SJ," he said.

Jonas Thomson, who had played his midget hockey in Indian Head that year, said having Sparvier, who was playing with the Yorkton Terriers of the Saskatchewan Junior Hockey League, was a real asset to the team. "He was kind of a leader for us up there coming from junior." The team didn't have a lot of time together before heading to Ontario, but jelled in a hurry. "Everyone knew each other. We'd all played against each other," said Thomson. "We knew we had to work as a team. It didn't take us long to do that — maybe by the end of the first game."

Travis Gardipy from Beardy's First Nation was 16 at the time of the championship and had been playing with Beardy's Blackhawks in the Saskatchewan AAA Midget Hockey League. He said having the Saskatchewan team in a tournament in Saskatoon a couple of weeks before heading to Ontario was a huge benefit. "We really came together there. It was a time to get our lines together and work on things," he offered.

Charlie Keshane, the team's head coach, noted the coaching staff was both surprised and pleased with how the team came together over only a handful of games. "It was surprising how competitive we were in the tournament," he said, adding that a loss in the final had some people, including a few of the players, worried they weren't prepared for a national tournament. "Even some of the kids weren't too sure they were ready to go to Ontario," he said. "We told them it would take a little while to click."

Justin Magnuson, who also played with the Beardy's Blackhawks during the season, said the loss in the tourney final was in retrospect a good thing. "Losing a game in that tournament helped us be better in the future," he said. The team came together in Ontario in a hurry.

Saskatchewan went through the tournament undefeated, winning five straight on the men's side of the draw leading up to the final. "It was tough. There were some tough teams there," said Thomson. "But we just skated hard and worked hard." Magnuson, who hails from Saskatoon, said he'd felt confident to the point that he expected to go through the tournament without a loss, yet he also recognized there were good teams to beat. "Southern Ontario was a good team, very skilled," he offered as an example.

Keshane said again that the coaches were pleased by the results. "We were very surprised we did so well, especially judging from the Saskatoon tournament. But we jelled quite quickly... They came together so quickly." The coach said a key to the team becoming so close-knit in such a short time was involving the players not just in practices, but in off-ice activities as well.

The toughest game, though, came in the final, against Manitoba. "They were very good," said Gardipy. "They had quite a few junior A players on their team." Keshane, too, noted his charges would be in for a tough go in the final game. "They (Manitoba) were the powerhouse there. They had a lot of junior A and junior B players. They had a really strong core of hockey players and were defending champs." So going in, Keshane wanted only one thing, "110 per cent from the players," and as long as that was there, he would accept either winning or losing.

Sparvier pointed out that it was a game with a weird ending. "That was a crazy game," he said. "We were down 2-1 with two seconds left." Sparvier said Manitoba thought they had it won until a player grabbed the puck inside the crease area, giving Saskatchewan a penalty shot. Keshane said it was obviously a huge break for Saskatchewan, on a penalty some officials call and others let go. "It was fortunate for us the ref called it." Magnuson said it felt as though the Saskatchewan team was destined to prevail. "I don't know if it was luck or fate. It was probably a bit of both."

With a penalty shot to take, Keshane began looking down the bench for Magnuson, who had had a couple of breakaways in the tournament and done well. But as Keshane looked to centre ice, Gardipy was already standing on the dot. "He had kind of been fighting the puck in the game," said the coach. For his part, Gardipy said he just had a gut feeling he was the one to take the critical shot. "I just went straight to centre ice. I thought I could score," he said, adding that the coaches went with his hunch. "I thought I'd been playing really well throughout the tournament and that I had a chance to score." The confidence Keshane saw in Gardipy's move to centre ice was enough for him. "He was standing at the dot focusing. I thought, he wants it, so let him go. I didn't even watch the play. I turned my head away and waited."

With the gold medal on the line, the young Gardipy just tried to stay focused on what he had to do. "I just tried to block out all the fans. I was thinking of the move I was going to do on the goalie." Gardipy went in on the net, faked once and shot a forehand along the ice — and the red light went on. "It was relief, and get ready for overtime," he said.

"They had the game won," said Thomson, who noted there was less than three seconds on the clock when the penalty was called. Gardipy's goal renewed the team's fire. In overtime, Magnuson was set free on a breakaway less than five minutes in, scoring to give the Saskatchewan team the win. "I just remember I was at the end of my shift. I was a little slow on the backcheck," he said. "I got the puck on a fast breakout." From there it was up to Magnuson, who got past the Manitoba defence and in on goal. "I saw the goalie was kind of far back in his net, so I decided to shoot and it went in."

Sparvier was also instrumental in the victory, setting up both Saskatchewan's first goal and the overtime winner in the final. "It was fun. I got to do some stuff I never got to before," he added, pointing to his increased offensive role on the team.

Keshane called the game the highlight of his coaching career to that point, adding that the joy he felt was for his young team. In some cases, he said, the players came from isolated communities and the opportunities to play on the national stage were limited. While some were expected to go on to junior, college and professional hockey, for "a handful of kids, that was the best they would get," he said. For the coaching staff, the training camp might have been the hardest part of the process, having only three days to select a team. "It was difficult for the staff to come up with a good core of hockey players in such a short time," said Keshane, adding that, fortunately, many players were coming out of competitive midget programs to start with.

Sparvier explained the team held a tryout camp at Beardy's just before Christmas and he was informed shortly after that he had made the team. Thomson said the tryout was in some ways intimidating, with roughly 100 players in attendance, yet he went into it feeling confident. "I played with and against a bunch of the guys," he said, adding that he'd been told that if he worked hard, he had a good shot at making the team. Thomson said coaches told him they liked his speed, aggressiveness and puck control, three aspects of his game that helped him earn a spot on the team.

For Thomson, who began skating at about three years of age, the tournament was his first time playing hockey outside Saskatchewan. At 17, he said he took that pretty much in stride. "As long as I was playing a sport I liked, it was good. I just wanted to enjoy it while I was there." Looking at the tournament and the championship win, he said it was certainly among the highlights of his hockey career to date. The only thing that comes close to the championship as far as a highlight went was making the Yorkton Terriers roster in the SJHL after their camp in the fall of 2003.

For Gardipy, whose goal breathed life into the team, it was a game to remember. "I think it's one of my biggest moments," he said, adding that playing in the Canada Winter Games in New Brunswick also rated highly. Yet he remembers the gold-medal celebration vividly too. "We all jumped on the ice and went crazy. We were all pretty happy with the victory, knowing we had beat a tough team who were defending champions, too."

Sparvier called the Aboriginal crown a definite highlight event. "It was pretty big," he said. "It was my last minor hockey and I went out with a win. And my dad was coaching (as an assistant), which made it that much better."

## Another Colour Man
*William Robertson*

Hey CBC, the guy I want to hear from
is the backup goalie, you know, what's-his-name.
My kids have had his card forever
traded it half a dozen times
I still can't remember his name
but I know his face, familiar
as beer ads, a smile without a name,
without a voice. Each intermission
some poor panting winger who's played
12:21 of the last twenty gasps
his blades-eye view of the game,
half of which he missed he was
so damn busy: crashes into his bench
sucking hard, head jerking, grabs
a quick squirt from a water bottle
force-feeds his muscles
oxygen, two guys hanging over
the glass, screaming at him,
shakes off sprays of sweat
from his scarred eyebrows, his twisted nose,
vaults the boards to the game.

But our man, the backup goalie,
sees it all, up and down the ice,
wincing with each shot—both nets—the crouched figure he could be,
sees the hits, passes that work,
hears the coaches shout, the trainer talking
as he tears and slaps adhesive, two guys
screaming some shit about who's chicken

it's this guy, Hockey Night in Canada, 82 games
a year plus practice, all he wants to do
is play, this is the guy I want
to hear from, stick
that microphone
in his face

## End of the Season
*William Robertson*

Now that it's down
to two teams
the games come only
every second night.
my wife's been away
seems like weeks
with weeks yet to go
even the yardwork's done
I feel bereft
these off nights
skaters regain their legs
workers repair the ice
I walk between the kitchen
and the exhausted newspaper
the telephone, the front door no one
comes to, but my wife
in nine days' time
probably the night of the cup:
she'll whistle down that TV set
call a fight then make up
a couple of hours in the penalty box
I'll forget hockey and all
that icy stuff

# A Hall of Our Own
*Darrell Davis*

Bernie Federko's hockey career is memorialized inside the Hockey Hall of Fame, a beautiful shrine located in a stately former bank building in downtown Toronto. Long before his 2002 induction into the Hall, Federko's achievements were well-known and proudly displayed in Foam Lake, Saskatchewan. Drive along Highway 16, the northerly Trans-Canada Highway known as the Yellowhead because of its eventual path through the Rocky Mountains, and about midway into the 1,100-kilometre drive between Lloydminster and Winnipeg is Federko's hometown. At the entrance to the Foam Lake Golf & Country Club sits a wooden one-storey building that serves as a clubhouse, a visitors information booth and a place to register for overnight stays at the nearby campground. At one end of the gravel parking lot is a large billboard, adorned with a pink ribbon, which reads "Proud to be Home of the Breast Friends," a group of women—including breast-cancer survivors—from Foam Lake who have raised $1.4 million for cancer research through sales of their cookbooks.

At the other end of the parking lot are laudatory posters of four hockey players and a sign that reads "Foam Lake Hockey Heroes: Dedicated in recognition of the individuals from this community who have achieved national and international stature in professional hockey."

It's a traditional practice across Western Canada for cities, towns and villages to honour their sports heroes with signage: In Langenburg, just down the Yellowhead from Foam Lake, former Edmonton Oilers captain Kelly Buchberger has a sign, though it's less conspicuous than the sign commending his sister Kerri, a longtime member of the Canadian women's volleyball team. In Foxwarren, Manitoba, they have signs feting hometown NHLers Pat Falloon, Ron Low and Mark Wotton. Also on the Yellowhead is Saltcoats, which hasn't produced an NHL player but is sign-worthy proud of world-champion curlers Joan (Inglis) McCusker and Steve Laycock.

Foam Lake's Hockey Heroes display celebrated the careers of Pat Elynuik, Ted Hargreaves, Dennis Polonich and Bernie Federko. Elynuik won the 1985 Memorial Cup with the WHL's Prince Albert Raiders, was a first-round draft choice of the Winnipeg Jets, played 506 regular-season games and earned 342 points with four NHL teams — Winnipeg, Washington, Tampa Bay and Ottawa — before retiring in 1997. Hargreaves won a bronze medal with Canada's hockey team at the 1968 Olympics and played one season with the World Hockey Association's Jets, but never appeared in the NHL. Polonich, an eighth-round draft choice by Detroit in 1973, played junior for the WCHL's Flin Flon Bombers and eventually played 390 regular-season NHL games, amassing 1,242 penalty minutes, with the Red Wings. Federko is the biggest star of the four Foam Lake honourees.

In 1975-76, his third and final year of junior hockey, Bernie Federko amassed 72 goals and 115 assists in 72 games with the Saskatoon Blades, giving him 344 points in 206 WCHL games. Federko was drafted seventh overall by the St. Louis Blues and began his pro career in the minors, but got summoned to The Show during his first season out of junior. He evolved into such an offensive talent that three seasons later he recorded 95 points for St. Louis. He eventually tallied 1,130 points on 369 goals and 761 assists in 1,000 NHL games over the course of 13 seasons in St. Louis and a final campaign, 1989-90, with Detroit. A shifty centre capable of making his teammates better, Federko's notoriety suffered because the Blues never advanced further than the semifinals, coming closest to a Stanley Cup finals appearance with a seventh-game 2-1 loss against the Calgary Flames in a 1986 divisional final. He was often described as one of the league's most underrated players. He was not underrated in St. Louis, however. Less than a year after he retired, the Blues retired Federko's sweater number 24. Ten years later, he was voted into the Hockey Hall of Fame. But no matter how far you go, when you're a Saskatchewan kid, you remember the early days.

"We had a great building in Foam Lake; the rink was right across the street from us," Federko said via telephone from St. Louis in October 2012. "When I was six or seven years old, it burned down. That was a sad day and I remember people with their hoses out, hosing down our house across the street so it wouldn't burn. It took two or three years to build another rink, a nice one with a curling rink. It was seven or eight blocks away, in town. In the meantime, Dad flooded the garden every year. There wasn't a lot of ponds or sloughs around, not around the Foam Lake area. Dad would put two-by-fours around the garden. We'd shovel the snow. By the end of the winter we would have snow piled about eight feet tall! It would be great because the pucks never left the yard. We would find some pucks every spring after the snow melted. We'd take the hose out and re-flood it when the ice got roughed up. We'd spend hours and hours out there. The yards weren't really that big. We'd play under the light from the back of the house, me and my three brothers. A lot of the boys in town were closer to my older brothers' age. At my age there were more girls than boys, so I actually played more with my brothers' friends than my friends, even though they were all spread out and not close to our house in our little town.

"We played street hockey. If we weren't in the backyard, we were out on the street, putting chunks of snow or stones to mark the goals. We played on grid roads, but there was so much snow, they didn't grade it off, cars drove over it. We had streetlights — one was one house down and the other was the other way, one house down. It was so shiny we could have played all night long if we were on the road because the streetlights were so bright. The puck would slide really well because the road was smooth from all the cars going over it. It was like ice."

Federko had just visited Saskatchewan before this conversation took place. He had gone to Saskatoon to see his family and friends, so the Blades piggybacked his visit into a promotional tour to remind hockey fans that the 2013 Memorial Cup, the championship of the 60 major junior hockey teams in Canada and the U.S., where eight of the franchises are located, was being played in Saskatoon's Credit Union Centre. As the host team, the Blades were granted an automatic berth in the tournament along with the winners of the Western Hockey League, Ontario Hockey League and Quebec Major Junior Hockey League.

Although Federko settled with his family in St. Louis after his playing career and didn't return to Saskatchewan too often, he found himself staying in touch with his home province through his television job as a hockey analyst for Blues games.

"I think it's somewhat of a fraternity — I still follow the guys from Saskatchewan and the guys who played for the Blades," said Federko. "When somebody comes through here, the first thing I look at when I'm looking through the rosters is, Where are they from or where did they play junior? If somebody comes from the same place as you, especially if it's Saskatchewan, it's a great place to grow up, so the roots we have in Saskatchewan and the way we're brought up, from Elmer Lach to all of us, are real. We're brought up in families that are real, who care about each other. We're all honest about where we're trying to go. We all look at Saskatchewan as being a big part of our lives.

"You start with something, you get an opportunity and you get the benefit of the doubt because you're working your tail off. If you make it, the people of Saskatchewan are very happy that you did make it.

"It's been a long time. I've been away for 36 years now. My mom's in Saskatoon, my dad passed away in January after 92 great years. He got pneumonia and couldn't fight through it; it was very short. I was up to see him in early January because he wasn't feeling very well. It was nice to be there. My wife's mom is there. We're all really close families. I also saw some guys I hadn't seen for a long time. We still get back there once in a while, but our family's lifestyles keep us here for most of the time. It's still home. (St. Louis) is home for us now; our children were born and raised here. But our home is still Saskatchewan. I don't get to Foam Lake very often because Mom and Dad moved out of there about 25 years ago. It's still where I got my start."

Federko was invited back to his home province to attend induction ceremonies in the summer of 2013 for the Saskatchewan Hockey Hall of Fame. He was part of the class that also included Clark Gillies of Moose Jaw, who won four Stanley Cups with the New York Islanders; Gordon "Red" Berenson of Regina, who played for the Regina Pats and the University of Michigan before embarking on a 17-year NHL career and returning to coach at Michigan; and Eddie Shore, who was born in Fort Qu'Appelle, grew up on a farm near Cupar and was known as "Old Blood and Guts" for the ferocity that helped him win the 1929 and 1939 Stanley Cups with Boston and be named the NHL's most valuable player four times during a 14-year career.

The builders inducted in 2013 were Del Wilson of Regina, a former owner and general manager of the Pats who helped form the Western Canada Junior Hockey League, and Bill Hay of Saskatoon, who played for the Pats and Colorado College en route to an NHL career in which he won the Calder Trophy as the league's top rookie in 1960 and the next year's Stanley Cup with Chicago. Hay later served as president of Hockey Canada and the Calgary Flames before becoming a chairman of the Hockey Hall of Fame, a role he relinquished in 2013. John Maddia of Indian Head, a former president of the Saskatchewan Amateur Hockey Association, was inducted as a grassroots builder and Michael (Mick) McGeough of Regina, who worked more than 1,000 NHL games as a referee, was inducted as an official. The lone team inducted was the 1914 Regina Victorias, who won the Allan Cup as Canada's top senior team in their first year of existence.

It's really quite a remarkable group of inductees for such a small province. And think about this—this was the second group of inductees! Shore, Federko and Gillies are in the Hockey Hall of Fame. Shore is in the Canadian Hall of Fame. For logistical and a few other reasons, they waited a year for their enshrinement because the huge inaugural class of inductees was even more impressive: Hockey Hall of Famers Gordie Howe, Bryan Trottier, Sid Abel, Elmer Lach, Max and Doug Bentley, Johnny Bower, Glenn Hall and builders Athol Murray, Ed Chynoweth and Gordon Juckes. Other players inducted in 2012 were Fred Sasakamoose and Metro Prystai, who played 11 years in the NHL and won two Stanley Cups with Detroit. The other builders were Bill Hunter, former Calgary Flames co-owner Daryl "Doc" Seaman and grassroots organizer Bill Ford. Dennis Pottage, a former referee-in-chief for the Canadian Hockey Association, was the official. The inducted teams were the 1973-74 Regina Pats, 1984-85 Prince Albert Raiders, 1988-89 Swift Current Broncos—all Memorial Cup champions—plus the 1982-83 CIAU-winning University of Saskatchewan Huskies and an era of the Semans Wheat Kings that won five league championships and five provincial intermediate C crowns between 1955 and 1964.

Before 2012 there was no special way of honouring Saskatchewan's hockey royalty. There is the Saskatchewan Sports Hall of Fame and Museum, which inducts hockey players, builders and teams as part of its annual ceremonies and which has encouraged cities like Saskatoon, Regina and Prince Albert to establish their own Halls of Fame to honour hometown sports heroes. But despite the abundance of famous, talented and influential people from Saskatchewan scattered throughout the hockey world, the Saskatchewan Hockey Association had not established its own Hall of Fame until Marc Habscheid prompted it. Habscheid, a former NHL player who also coached Canada's national team and several junior teams, including the Kelowna Rockets when they won the Memorial Cup in 2004, started thinking that his province should set up its own shrine in Swift Current, his hometown and a strong hockey community located on the Trans-Canada Highway on the route from Regina to Calgary.

"The funny thing about this is when I approached a few people about a Hall of Fame, there were some people interested but they didn't know each other," said Habscheid. "I said, 'Trust me, you'll all fit.' They did. And lots of people worked very hard to get it done."

The Saskatchewan Hockey Association jumped fully on board with the idea, supported by the Saskatchewan Sports Hall of Fame and Museum. SHA general manager Kelly McClintock helped assemble a board of directors and the committees necessary to run the Hall. Swift Current donated a site in its hockey arena, home of the WHL's Broncos, which was called the Civic Centre before being renamed the Credit Union iPlex. A room was set aside to house displays featuring jerseys, sticks, programs, testimonials and pictures of the inductees. When the Hall opened, even Marc Habscheid was impressed with what he learned about Saskatchewan's hockey history.

"There's a respect within the province for the game of hockey," he said. "It needed a Hockey Hall of Fame. This is so great to see... so much history involved and now it's coming to the forefront. I had no idea Johnny Bower and Elmer Lach were from Saskatchewan. To see people come back and what it means to them is spectacular. Right now Saskatchewan has about a million people; in years past, there was even less. To have the impact that

Gordie Howe or Glenn Hall or some of those builders have had, it's impressive for a province this size."

Saskatchewan's contributions to the NHL continue to be impressive. Quanthockey.com, perhaps the most current of the websites tracking Saskatchewan-born NHL players, showed 47 of them appeared in NHL games during the lockout-shortened 2012-13 season — 11 from Saskatoon, 10 from Regina, 11 from other cities and 14 who were born in small towns, villages or rural settings.

Knowing that three of the rural players were actually born in big cities, that means there were 17 current players who grew up in rural communities. Using those adjusted numbers, 64 percent of the players from Saskatchewan in the NHL are from cities, which is a reflection of the province as a whole. According to the 2012 census, there were 1,072,082 residents of the province—65 per cent is urban population and 35 per cent is rural population. They're all entwined, anyway. People from the cities depend on the farming economy, rural dwellers drop into the cities for entertainment and shopping. They know each other's business. It's a common refrain that everyone in Saskatchewan knows about the crops, the legislature and the Roughriders, and everyone has an opinion about those topics. They also follow extremely closely the fortunes of the Saskatchewan kids in the NHL.

Among fans who follow the exploits of the new generation of NHLers are well-known former players like Orland Kurtenbach, who was inducted into the Saskatchewan Sports Hall of Fame in 2012. When the NHL expanded into Vancouver in 1970, Kurtenbach became the team's first captain, an appropriate appointment considering that the Cudworth, Saskatchewan, native had played some semi-pro hockey in Vancouver between stints in the NHL.

As a kid Kurtenbach lived on a farm near Cudworth before moving with his family to Prince Albert, where he overcame early skating deficiencies, played junior hockey and was scouted by the New York Rangers. He had to work for everything he got.

"We moved off the farm and got there when I was 11 years old," said Kurtenbach. "I couldn't make a team because I couldn't skate. I had old skates; they looked like goalie skates. At that time, with the outdoor rinks, when you had a chance you would play and play and play. I caught up. In about four or five years, what really helped me was playing with the senior team that we had locally; it had some ex-juniors. That really helped me. The next year I played junior with the (Prince Albert) Mintos and I was the rookie of the year. That was really a big, big help to me. I was playing against grown men. They kicked the tar out of you. It wasn't dirty, but when you were fighting for the puck, you were fighting against a grown man. You have no strength compared to them. I was 16. I went to the Rangers camp in Saskatoon. At that time there was a loose affiliation between the NHL and juniors. Flin Flon was sort of involved with the Rangers as well; they were able to pick me up for the Memorial Cup in 1956-57. I turned pro the next year with the Vancouver Canucks in the Western League. You had guys like Guyle Fielder, Phil Maloney. I went to the Buffalo Bisons (American Hockey League) the next year—there was Willie Marshall and Dunc Fisher. They weren't very big guys. But Guyle Fielder was the closest thing to a Wayne Gretzky in terms of handling the puck. I'm not too sure he wanted to be that type of player. From what I read he went up to Detroit and they put him with (Ted) Lindsay and (Gordie) Howe. There's no way—Gordie wanted the puck. I sort of felt the same way: I wanted the puck. Guyle's not going to have the puck when Gordie's there."

Kurtenbach went on to play 639 games in the NHL with the Rangers, Bruins, Leafs and finally the Canucks, when for their 1970-71 NHL debut he tallied 53 points in 52 games. He added 61, 28 and 21 points in three subsequent seasons before retiring. He had the opportunity to extend his career but declined an offer to join the World Hockey Association. Though he never played in the WHA, he appreciates what the upstart league did for players' salaries.

"The NHL didn't market the way they do now. Our wages were shitty. They finally got it off the ground, but it didn't really go until the World Hockey Association came in and Bobby Hull signed with Winnipeg. I was fishing with Bobby and Andy Bathgate about three, four years ago on the West Coast. Bobby said, 'I would have stayed in Chicago for $600,000, but they wouldn't go for it.' I think he was making $400,000. (Blackhawks owner Bill) Wirtz wouldn't budge. Our wages didn't really start till about 1992-93. When we played in that old six-team league for those shitty wages, it was a no-win situation other than playing for pride and the fact you made more money than the average person, but not a helluva lot more. When I was making minimum wage of $7,000 in Boston, there was guys at home making $4,500 or $5,500."

One of the benefits of having a Hockey Hall of Fame in Saskatchewan is that it provides the occasion to bring hockey greats like Bernie Federko and Orland Kurtenbach together, to hear their take on the game of today and yesteryear and to have these and other keen observers discuss what makes Saskatchewan hockey players so special.

"I hate using the terms, but it's usually grit and heart, they just don't give up. It comes from the soil," Graham Tuer said with a laugh while attending the Hall's 2012 induction ceremonies in Regina. "We always had to make our own entertainment, so we went to the rink and spent hours and hours there. That was true up until 20 years ago."

For nearly half a century, Tuer has been scouting minor-hockey players for major junior teams and the SHA. He believes Saskatchewan players will long be in demand by NHL teams, and the province is continuing to find ways to develop them.

"We're going to have fewer players because it costs so much. It's a tremendous amount of money for a parent to lay out for a kid to play hockey. I worked this week at our Western Prospects camp — we had 150 kids there from British Columbia, Northwest Territories, Texas, Colorado, Manitoba and Saskatchewan. A good bunch of kids. Like everything else, when you put it in a distribution curve, there are a few kids who don't really fit, but there are also some outstanding ones."

Tuer has certainly seen his share of prospects and players, including everyone in the group of Saskatchewan players who appeared in the NHL during the 2012-13 campaign. Here's that list from Quanthockey.com:

Patrick Marleau of Aneroid (San Jose), Brenden Morrow of Carlyle (Pittsburgh), Ryan Getzlaf of Regina (Anaheim), Scott Hartnell of Regina (Philadelphia), Wade Redden of Lloydminster (Boston), Chris Kunitz of Regina (Pittsburgh), Jarret Stoll of Melville (Los Angeles), Brooks Laich of Wawota (Washington), Curtis Glencross of Kindersley (Calgary), Colby Armstrong of

Lloydminster (Montreal), Brett Clark of Wapella (Minnesota), Jordan Eberle of Regina (Edmonton), Blake Comeau of Meadow Lake (Columbus), Cory Sarich of Saskatoon (Calgary), Nick Schultz of Strasbourg (Edmonton), Tyler Bozak of Regina (Toronto), Boyd Gordon of Unity (Phoenix), Travis Moen of Swift Current (Montreal), Luke Schenn of Saskatoon (Philadelphia), Derek Dorsett of Kindersley (New York Rangers), Darroll Powe of Saskatoon (New York Rangers), Zack Smith of Maple Creek (Ottawa), Brayden Schenn of Saskatoon (Philadelphia), Darcy Hordichuk of Kamsack (Edmonton), Tanner Glass of Regina (Pittsburgh), Sheldon Brookbank of Lanigan (Chicago), Dwight King of Meadow Lake (Los Angeles), Jared Cowen of Saskatoon (Ottawa), Jaden Schwartz of Melfort (St. Louis), Blair Jones of Central Butte (Calgary), Adam Cracknell of Prince Albert (St. Louis), Jordan Hendry of Nokomis (Anaheim), Brett Carson of Regina (Calgary), Tyson Strachan of Melfort (Florida), Keith Aulie of Rouleau (Tampa Bay), James Wright of Saskatoon (Winnipeg), Cam Ward of Saskatoon (Carolina), Brendan Mikkelson of Regina (Tampa Bay), Nolan Yonkman of Punnichy (Florida), Eric Gryba of Saskatoon (Ottawa), Dan Ellis of Saskatoon (Carolina), Steve MacIntyre of Brock (Pittsburgh), Braden Holtby of Lloydminster (Washington), Josh Harding of Regina (Minnesota), Devan Dubnyk of Regina (Edmonton), Darcy Kuemper of Saskatoon (Minnesota) and Sean Collins of Saskatoon (Columbus).

The players truly come from every corner of Saskatchewan, but it's not uncommon to have them bunched together, as Habscheid recalled from his days playing minor hockey.

"I grew up on a farm about 10 miles south of Swift Current," he said. "When I played bantam hockey in Swift Current, we had 15 players on the team. Years ago I counted after the fact that nine of them signed professional contracts. There was Rocky Trottier, Gord Kluzak, Lane Lambert, Mark Lamb, Stu Innes, Al Larochelle. It was incredible to see a small town produce that many players. At the time, we were just a bunch of kids playing together who didn't know what would happen. We didn't know any better. We played for the love of the game. Who's to say what would happen? I think it's the fact that for a lot of the kids, it was just a way of life. You lived and breathed it. It didn't matter if it was 50 below, if you found a puddle that had frozen over and was 10 yards around, you'd get the skates and go and play. You played hockey because you loved it, it was our fibre and we all understood it was such a privilege to be involved in the game."

Bryan Trottier's tiny hometown of Val Marie sits in the southwest corner of Saskatchewan, close to Swift Current; the ranch he grew up on is about 10 kilometres (six miles) from the Canada/U.S. border. Trottier recalls jokingly that his father's cattle would wander illegally into the U.S. on a daily basis.

"I have no clue why Saskatchewan produces so many hockey players," said Trottier, a winner of six Stanley Cups as a player — four with the New York Islanders and two with the Pittsburgh Penguins. But he does know, because he was one of them, one of the best. And he was speaking at festivities for the brand-new Saskatchewan Hockey Hall of Fame.

"It's something Saskatchewan should be proud of. Maybe it's the friendly, Prairie winters that allow us to have a lot of rinks and produce a lot of good players. There are lots of rinks per capita, a lot of ice for kids to get ice time. There's good coaching, good parents, good communities that support the hockey.

"Our little province has produced some great players and is rich in history at every level. All of our stories are a little different but for all of us it's really hard, because if it was easy, everybody would do it. It just makes a person appreciate it a little more. There are twists and turns and curves, but each one of us shares a common denominator: our Saskatchewan roots."

# Bios

**Bill Boyd** has covered two Winter Olympic Games and two world hockey championships for print and television. He was formerly a producer for CBC News and later for *The Fifth Estate*. His freelance writing has appeared in *Time*, *The Washington Post*, *Sports Illustrated* and *The Globe and Mail*.

**Kelley Jo Burke** is an award-winning playwright, poet and documentarian, a professor of theatre and creative writing, and was for many years host of CBC Radio's SoundXchange. Her plays include the national award-winning *Us* (with composer Jeff Straker), *The Selkie Wife* (Scirocco) and *Charming and Rose: True Love* (Blizzard). Her most recent documentaries for CBC Radio's IDEAS include *Bringing Up Furbaby* and *Shame on You(Tube)*. Burke lives in Regina.

**Mick Burrs** (a.k.a. Steven Michael Berzensky) is a Canadian poet who currently lives in Toronto. He was born and raised in California. After leaving the United States to avoid the Vietnam War, he spent much of his life in Yorkton, Saskatchewan. He won the 1998 Saskatchewan Book Award for Poetry for a volume of his collected Saskatchewan works, *Variations on the Birth of Jacob*. He is a former editor of *Grain* magazine.

**Lorna Crozier**, who was born in Swift Current, is the author of 16 books of poetry. She received the Governor General's Award for Poetry in 1992 and she is an officer of the Order of Canada. As a child growing up in a prairie community where the local heroes were hockey players and curlers, she "never once thought of being a writer." Now professor emerita at the University of Victoria, she conducts poetry workshops across the country.

**Robert Currie** from Moose Jaw is the author of eight poetry collections, two novels and two books of short stories. He served four years as Saskatchewan's third Poet Laureate and in 2009 received the Lieutenant Governor's Award for Lifetime Achievement in the Arts. He is sad to report that he last played organized hockey in Grade 6.

**Calvin Daniels** was born in Tisdale, Saskatchewan, and resides in Yorkton where he is an assistant editor and senior reporter with *Yorkton This Week*. His stories have been widely published and Daniels has won twelve Saskatchewan Weekly Newspapers Association awards. His love of hockey was galvanized by Paul Henderson's famous 1972 goal, and he has enjoyed covering the SJHL's Yorkton Terriers. With more than 25 years in the newspaper business, Daniels is the author of eight books.

**Darrell Davis** grew up skating on the same outdoor hockey rinks as Red Berenson, Dirk Graham and Doug Wickenheiser. His father Lorne won a Stanley Cup with the Montreal Canadiens before serving as a longtime scout with the St. Louis Blues and Edmonton Oilers. It is no small accident that with that pedigree Davis would go on to become one of the best sports journalists in the country. Davis is the author of *Fire On Ice*. He resides in Regina.

**Wes Fineday** from Sweetgrass First Nation is a Cree elder, traditional healer, ceremonialist, medicine person, songwriter and storyteller. He works as a traditional knowledge keeper and educator in various schools and universities. He also leads healing gatherings, fasting camps, and workshops for professional healers and traditional knowledge keepers from many different cultural backgrounds.

**Myrna Garanis** is an Edmonton essayist/poet claiming the same hometown as Gordie Howe. Her dad bought grain for the pool there, Myrna biked to Floral School for eight years and was confirmed in Floral Church. She's eyeing Floral Cemetery for a peaceful final rest. Until that moment, she'll continue work on an essay collection in which hockey and Gordie Howe pop up time and time again.

**Gerald Hill**, two-time winner of the Saskatchewan Book Award for Poetry, published his sixth poetry collection, *Hillsdale Book*, with NeWest Press, and *A Round for Fifty Years: A History of Regina's Globe Theatre* with Coteau Books, both in 2015. He was Poet Laureate of Saskatchewan in 2016. Gerald lives and writes in Regina.

**Gary Hyland** (1940-2011) from Moose Jaw, one of Saskatchewan's most dynamic poets, was a teacher, writer, activist, consultant and editor. He was the author of eight books, and founder of the Saskatchewan Festival of Words as well as being instrumental in the creation of the Moose Jaw Cultural Centre. Gary was a community organizer who got things done. He was an officer of the Order of Canada.

**Don Kerr**, professor emeritus in the English department at the University of Saskatchewan, is the author of five poetry collections, plays and short stories. He served on the Saskatoon Public Library board for eleven years, and as chair for five of those years. A former Poet Laureate of Saskatchewan, he was also the first chair of the Saskatoon Heritage Society.

**Randy Lundy** is a member of the Barren Lands (Cree) First Nation. Born in northern Manitoba, he has lived most of his life in Saskatchewan. He has published two previous books, *Under the Night Sun* and *Gift of the Hawk*, and 2018 will see the publication of a third book of poems, *Blackbird Song* from University of Regina Press. He teaches Indigenous literatures and creative writing at the University of Regina.

**Laurie Lynn Muirhead**, who lives on a farm near Shellbrook, Saskatchewan, writes what she lives and is especially inspired by the extreme simplicity of the natural world about her. Her work has appeared in *The New Quarterly* and *The Society* and broadcast on CBC Radio. Her first collection of poetry *Bone Sense* was published by Thistledown Press.

**Dolores Reimer** (1957-2013) was born in The Pas, Manitoba. She grew up at Big Trout Lake, Ontario, Fort Smith Northwest Territories and Cranbrook, British Columbia. She moved to Saskatchewan in 1986 and lived with her family in the historic Jacoby House in Dundurn on the Louis Riel Trail. A poet and fiction writer, Reimer, active in organizing minor hockey, was also a hockey commentator on CBC Saskatchewan radio and TV as well as a past president of the Saskatchewan Writers' Guild.

**William Robertson** published his fifth collection of poems, *Decoys* (Thistledown), in October 2017. He has also published a biography of k.d. lang (1992) and edited two collections of poetry by his creative writing students in the Indian Teacher Education Program at the University of Saskatchewan. He lives in Saskatoon.

**Mansel Robinson** has had over a dozen plays produced across the country, including *Street Wheat, Spitting Slag, Picking Up Chekhov, Bite the Hand* and *Two Rooms*. In 2018, he was one of the writers on a multilingual, multicultural revisionist historical extravaganza, *Gabriel Dumont's Wild West Show*. A longtime citizen of Saskatchewan, he now lives in Northern Ontario. For the record, Mansel was an enthusiastic bench-warmer in every sport he played.

**Allan Safarik**. His books include: *When Light Falls from the Sun*, winner of the 2005 Saskatchewan Book Award for Poetry, as well as *Bluebacks and Silver Brights: A Lifetime in the BC Fisheries From Bounty to Plunder* with his late father, Norman Safarik. His novel *Swedes' Ferry* has continued to be a bestseller on the prairies since its publication in 2013. Safarik, along with his late wife Dolores Reimer, edited three hockey books in the Arsenal Pulp Press Little Red Books series including: *Quotations From Chairman Ballard, Quotations From Chairman Cherry*, and *Quotations On The Great One*.

**Stephen Scriver** was first known as "The Hockey Poet" with the publishing of his three books of poems about small-town hockey in Saskatchewan. His play about the Second World War, *Letters In Wartime*, co-written with Kenneth Brown, has been staged across Canada. He has also researched and written documentaries for History Television. He lives a solitary life in his hometown of Wolseley, Saskatchewan, where he is a town councillor and local archivist.

**Glen Sorestad** was Canada's first provincially appointed Poet Laureate; he served as Poet Laureate of Saskatchewan from 2000 to 2004. He has published over 20 volumes of poetry and appeared in over 70 anthologies, textbooks and other non-fiction works. His poems have been translated into eight languages. Sorestad and his wife Sonia were original founders of Thistledown Press and he was Thistledown's president until they both retired from publishing in 2000.

**Rudy Thauberger**, born in Saskatoon, grew up in Saskatoon, Regina and Victoria, B.C. He wrote the screenplays for the feature films *The Rhino Brothers* and *Chicago Heights* (with Daniel Nearing), as well as the short film *Goalie* (based on his short story) and the Syfy movies of the week *Snowmageddon* and *The 12 Disasters of Christmas*. He holds an MFA in creative writing from the University of British Columbia and works as an instructor at the Vancouver Film School.

**Maureen Ulrich**, who was born in Saskatoon and grew up in Calgary and Edmonton, is a Young Adult author and playwright who resides in Lampman, Saskatchewan. Passionate about sports, she can often be found at a diamond, rink or football field. Her story in this anthology is an excerpt from her Young Adult hockey novel *Breakway* (Coteau), her third hockey novel for teens. It follows *Face Off* and the first book of the series, *Power Plays*.

**Brenda Zeman**, a former elite athlete, became an anthropologist, journalist and author. In her Canadian bestseller *To Run With Longboat*, she fused oral history, story and invention in the docufiction genre. She co-authored *88 Years of Puck Chasing In Saskatchewan*. She was a writer/broadcaster, a documentary writer and playwright at CBC Radio. At the Saskatchewan Sports Hall of Fame she was a cultural historian. She founded and led the award-winning program Crossing Bridges: Bridge City Track and Arts Program at the Saskatoon Tribal Council.

# Permissions

Bill Boyd's essays, *Indian Head, Saskatchewan* and *Bienfait, Saskatchewan*, reprinted from *Hockey Towns: Stories of Small Town Hockey in Canada*, Doubleday Canada. By permission of the author.
Kelley Jo Burke's poem, *At the Arena*, reprinted from *Going Top Shelf*, Heritage House Publishing. By permission of the author.
Mick Burrs' (a.k.a. Steven Michael Berzensky) poem, *My First Hockey Service*, reprinted from *That Sign of Perfection*, Black Moss Press. By permission of the author.
Lorna Crozier's poem, *Canadian Angels*, commissioned by CBC Radio's *Sounds Like Canada*. By permission of the author.
Robert Currie's story, *Max Bentley and the Hockey Pants*, reprinted from *Between the Lines: A Journal of Hockey Literature*. By permission of the author. Robert Currie's poems: *Hockey Night*, *Hockey Lesson* and *Beneath the Frozen Moon*. By permission of the author.
Calvin Daniels's essays, *Saskatchewan's Old Golden Girls* and *Aboriginal Title Comes to a Young Team*, reprinted from *Guts and Go; Great Saskatchewan Hockey Stories*, Heritage House Publishing. By permission of Heritage House Publishing. Calvin Daniels's story, *The Woman Behind the Mask*, reprinted from *Skating the Edge*, Thistledown Press. By permission of Thistledown Press.
Darrell Davis's essay, *A Hall of Our Own*, reprinted from *Fire on Ice*, MacIntyre Purcell Publishing. By permission of the author.
Wes Fineday's story, *The Hockey Game*, reprinted from *Achimoona*, Fifth House. By permission of the author.
Myrna Garanis's poem, *Gordie Howe Statue, Saskatoon*, reprinted from *Between the Lines: A Journal of Hockey Literature*. By permission of the author.
Gerald Hill's poem, *Anecdote of the Hockey Game*, reprinted from *Going Top Shelf*, Heritage House Publishing. By permission of the author.
Gary Hyland's poem, *The B- P- T*, reprinted from *Going Top Shelf*, Heritage House Publishing. By permission of Sharon Nichvalodoff. Gary Hyland's poem, *Northland Pro*, reprinted from *That Sign of Perfection*, Black Moss Press. By permission of Sharon Nichvalodoff.

Don Kerr's poems, *Gordie's Floral Sky* and *Art is International and has No Borders*, reprinted from *Between the Lines: A Journal of Hockey Literature*. By permission of the author.

Randy Lundy's story, *Autumn 1972*, reprinted from *Between the Lines: A Journal of Hockey Literature*. By permission of the author.

Laurie Muirhead's poem, *Farm Team*, reprinted from *Between the Lines: A Journal of Hockey Literature*. By permission of the author.

Dolores Reimer's story, *The Shut Out*, reprinted from *That Sign of Perfection*, Black Moss Press. By permission of Allan Safarik.

William Robertson's poems, *In Plain Sight* and *End of the Season*, reprinted from *Between the Lines: A Journal of Hockey Literature*." By permission of the author.

William Robertson's poem, *Another Colour Man*. By permission of the author.

Mansel Robinson's story, *Hockey Nights in Canada*, reprinted from *Between the Lines: A Journal of Hockey Literature*. By permission of the author.

Allan Safarik's story, *The Northfield Comets*, reprinted from *That Sign of Perfection*, Black Moss Press. By permission of the author.

Stephen Scriver's poems, *Wreck League*, *Once Is Once Too Many*, *Stanislowski Vs. Grenfell* and *Johnny*, reprinted from *Sundog Highway*, by Coteau Books. By permission of the author.

Glen Sorestad's poems, *Old Hockey Skates* and *Old-timers Hockey*, reprinted from *Between the Lines: A Journal of Hockey Literature*. By permission of the author.

Rudy Thauberger's story, *Goalie*, reprinted from *Words On Ice*, Key Porter Books. By permission of the author.

Maureen Ulrich's story, *Breakaway* (an excerpt), reprinted from *Breakaway*, Coteau Books. By permission of the author.

Brenda Zeman's story, *The Reluctant Black Hawk*, reprinted from *Sundog Highway*, Coteau Books. By permission of the author.

# Acknowledgements

Publishing is a collaborative effort. With thanks to Landon Johnson, John MacIntyre, Vernon Oickle, Emily Safarik and Caroline Walker.

Other books by Allan Safarik include *When Light Falls from the Sun* (winner of the 2005 Saskatchewan book award for poetry) as well as the acclaimed *Bluebacks and Silver Brights: A Lifetime in the BC Fisheries From Bounty to Plunder*, which he co-wrote with his late father, Norman Safarik, and the novel, *Swedes' Ferry*. A lifelong hockey fan, Safarik has spent the past 30 years following hockey in Saskatchewan.